D0877032

LATER
GATOR

A Miss Fortune Mystery

NEW YORK TIMES BESTSELLING AUTHOR

JANA DELEON

GM

Copyright © 2016 Jana DeLeon

All rights reserved. This copy is intended for the original purchaser of this book. No part of this book may be reproduced, scanned, or distributed in any printed or electronic form without prior written permission from the author except by reviewers who may quote brief excerpts in connection with a review. Please do not participate in or encourage piracy of copyrighted materials in violation of the author's rights. Purchase only authorized editions.

If you've never read a Miss Fortune mystery, you can start with LOUISIANA LONGSHOT, the first book in the series. If you prefer to start with this book, here are a few things you need to know.

Fortune Redding – a CIA assassin with a price on her head from one of the world's most deadly arms dealers. Because her boss suspects that a leak at the CIA blew her cover, he sends her to hide out in Sinful, Louisiana, posing as his niece, a librarian and ex–beauty queen named Sandy-Sue Morrow.

Ida Belle and Gertie – served in the military in Vietnam as spies, but no one in the town is aware of that fact except Fortune and Deputy LeBlanc.

Sinful Ladies Society – local group founded by Ida Belle, Gertie, and deceased member Marge. In order to gain membership, women must never have married or if widowed, their husband must have been deceased for at least ten years.

Sinful Ladies Cough Syrup – sold as an herbal medicine in Sinful, which is dry, but it's actually moonshine manufactured by the Sinful Ladies Society.

Chapter One

I stabbed my fork into a stack of blueberry pancakes and shoved a huge chunk into my mouth, savoring the explosion of flavor. Francine's pancakes should be a controlled substance. It was impossible to stop eating them once you got a taste.

"Must be good," Gertie said. "I haven't worn that expression since the last time I enjoyed the company of a man. I need to give my face muscles a workout soon."

Ida Belle rolled her eyes. "You haven't enjoyed the company of a man in so many years, those muscles in your face have atrophied."

I swallowed and took a big sip of coffee. "In so many ways, pancakes are better than a man. They don't require any complicated relationship maneuvering. You don't have to clean your house, or put on good underwear or makeup to hang out with them, and when you're done, they never pester you to call."

Gertie shook her head. "I'm convinced you're a man hiding out in a woman's body."

"Nah," Ida Belle said. "Fortune is tougher than any man. She's just a woman without female trappings."

"If Fortune didn't have any female trappings, Carter wouldn't be trying to hit it again," Gertie said.

"Hit it?" Ida Belle asked.

"Get lucky," Gertie said. "Don't you people ever listen to rap? I swear with you two, it's like living in pioneer days."

"And you would know that firsthand," Ida Belle said.

I laughed, and realized how happy I was to hear that sound. Things had been really odd for a couple weeks. The CIA's attempt to take down Ahmad, the man who wanted me dead, had failed, leaving me with no option but to continue with my deep cover in Sinful and forcing me to do a lot of soul-searching about how I wanted to structure the rest of my life, particularly my career. Then I'd done something reflexive and Carter had figured out I wasn't really a librarian. Once he knew the truth, he'd dumped me, which I'd always guessed was coming. The part I hadn't figured on was how awful I would feel or how much I would miss him.

Just when I thought my life couldn't get any more miserable, things started to change for the better. First of all, Carter had decided that my lies to him aside, he missed me as well, and even though our relationship was probably completely ill-advised, we were going to ignore conventional wisdom and give it another go. Second, I'd finally made a partial decision about my career. When this was over and I was free to be Fortune Redding again, it wasn't going to be with the CIA. Unfortunately, I had absolutely zero idea what I wanted to do with myself, which had led to this breakfast meeting with Ida Belle and Gertie.

"So let's address the reason for this breakfast," Ida Belle said.

"We just talked about the pancakes," Gertie said.

Ida Belle stared at the ceiling for several seconds. I was pretty sure when she did that she was asking God for patience, or maybe to prevent her from opening fire. Finally, she looked back at Gertie. "The pancakes are the reason for having breakfast *here*. This is about Fortune's career. Remember?"

"Oh yeah, that," Gertie said. "Well, it would help if we

knew where she wanted to live. I mean, if you want to be a marine biologist but live in Idaho, it's not optimum."

"I think we're safe on the marine biologist gig," I said, "and Idaho."

"As much as I hate to admit it," Ida Belle said, "Gertie does make a point. Have you considered where you'll live?"

Gertie bounced up and down in her seat like a child with one hand in the air and repeated "pick here" over and over again until Ida Belle threw a sausage link at her.

"I wish I knew," I said. "I mean, you guys are great and don't think I haven't thought about staying here, but what if Carter and I don't work out? Then I'm stuck here, running into my ex every day. I don't think I'd enjoy that much."

"Okay," Gertie said, "I'm not even going to argue about how perfect you and Carter are for each other. Instead, I'm going to approach this from a practical standpoint."

"This I gotta hear," Ida Belle mumbled into her coffee cup.

Gertie glared at her, then looked back at me. "How are you fixed financially? Obviously, Sinful doesn't have the salary to offer you at a job that you could probably command in DC, so it's something that definitely factors into your choices."

Ida Belle lowered her coffee cup. "That's actually a good point. I mean, if you don't mind telling us your personal business."

I laughed. "You've seen me naked. Why would I care if you know about money? That's the least of the things I try to keep a secret."

"So how are you positioned?" Ida Belle asked.

"Really good," I said. "I inherited a good amount of money when my dad died, and a house I sold for triple what my parents paid for it. They both had nice life insurance policies, and I make a decent salary. Combine that with the fact that I have limited free time and the only thing I spend money on is a one-bedroom apartment and weapons, and I'd say I could probably purchase a decent house and live for the next ten years without having to work at all."

"That's great!" Gertie said, both she and Ida Belle looking pleased. "That means you're not limited on location. So then the real question is, what do you want to do?"

I shook my head. "That's the problem. I don't know. I keep thinking about it over and over. I look around here and watch television and see people at work and try to imagine myself doing what they're doing and I can't. Well, except for when I was watching a Formula 1 race, but I don't think they're going to let me in one of those cars."

"Probably not," Ida Belle agreed, "but it's an excellent choice."

"When I was a teacher," Gertie said, "I used to tell my students to approach this question based on their talents."

"Yeah, I don't think you can get paid to kill people unless you work for the government," I said. "Not legally, anyway."

"You're selling yourself short," Gertie said. "I'm sure you have other talents. Maybe some you're not even aware that you have. A lot of these things are genetic. We know you followed in your father's footsteps at the CIA, but what about your mother? Did she work?"

I nodded. "She was an architect. She designed office buildings and parks and shopping centers and houses. I've gone to see everything she designed in person. They're all beautiful, with courtyards and flowers."

I felt a tug when I spoke about my mother. She'd died when I was young, and sometimes I was afraid my memories would fade. That I'd have nothing left to remember her by except pictures and those buildings she'd designed.

Gertie perked up. "An architect would be a great job. Between lunacy and hurricanes, there's always construction going on down here. We could become partners. You could design the buildings and I'd be the foreman."

Ida Belle stared at her. "Have you forgotten the time I helped you repair your shed and you shot me in the butt with the nail gun?"

"It was a finishing nail and I was five feet away," Gertie said. "It's not like I crippled you."

"Tell that to the Millers' cat," Ida Belle said.

"He walks fine with three legs," Gertie said.

Since I was pretty sure I'd never be able to maintain a liability insurance policy with Gertie on a job site, I figured that option was out. And then there was the part where I couldn't draw a straight line.

"It's not for me," I said. "I don't have that vision, or whatever they call it, that artists need to do their job."

"What about shrimping?" Gertie asked.

Ida Belle and I both stared at her as if she'd lost her mind.

"Why in the world would I want to be a shrimper?" I asked. "It's long, grueling work, the pay is dependent on the market, and I'd smell fishy all the time."

Gertie threw her hands in the air. "I'm just trying to think of things that would keep you here and wouldn't require you to work for anyone else. That might be problematic."

"I work for other people at the CIA," I said.

"Yes," Gertie said, "but they all have the same training you do. A regular civilian wouldn't stand a chance."

"She's got a point," Ida Belle said. "Not that I think you'd run around shooting bosses, but you're used to calling the shots and being independent. Whatever you do, you'd need to be in charge."

Gertie straightened in her chair, looking excited. "You could buy the Swamp Bar! I heard they're interested in selling."

"No way," I said. I'd already spent far too many embarrassing and awkward moments at that bar. I wasn't interested in creating legal ties.

Ida Belle sighed. "We're so stupid. The answer is right in front of our faces and we're sitting here talking about shrimp and bars."

Gertie and I looked at Ida Belle, waiting for her to reveal her thought of genius.

"You should be a private detective," Ida Belle said.

Gertie's jaw dropped a bit and she looked from Ida Belle to me, clearly enthralled with the idea. I had to admit, it wasn't bad as far as ideas went, at least in the imagining stage. But the reality stage was a completely different thing.

"Think about it," Ida Belle said. "You're already an expert at weapons, surveillance, and self-defense. You've got exceptional observation skills, and you're a logical thinker. Look at all the crimes you've solved since you've been in Sinful."

"A lot of those were luck," I said, "and in some cases, the solution arrived too late."

"You're not a superhero," Ida Belle said. "But you're more qualified for that job than any other, unless you want to work security detail for famous people."

"Pass," I said. The last thing I wanted to do was stand around holding purses with dogs and waiting on some twit to come out of a trendy dress shop.

But Ida Belle's idea had gotten my attention. I'd come across a couple of PIs in my CIA work, and I was positive I was more competent than either of them. And there were probably schools or something that I could attend to learn more about how to do the job, especially the legal end of things. The federal government wasn't as concerned about those things as nongovernment employees had to be.

"So?" Ida Belle asked.

"I don't know," I said. "I mean, I like the idea, and even though a bunch of it is probably boring as hell, I think I'd like the work for the most part."

"But?"

"But staying here and being a PI...and dating Carter."

Gertie whistled. "I hadn't thought about that. With all his 'no poking into police business' nonsense, he'd probably have a stroke if you set up shop to do exactly that."

"Probably," Ida Belle said, "but he'd get over it. As far as sins go, that would be one of the least Fortune has committed."

"Thanks a lot," I said.

"No disrespect," Ida Belle said. "I was right there with you hiding the truth and making up lies. And I don't blame either of us for a single one of them."

"The thing is," I said, "we've helped catch some criminals, but I'm pretty sure our methods aren't allowed."

"They are if no one finds out," Gertie said. "Isn't that the rule?"

"It is for a lot of people," Ida Belle said, "but I think you probably need to make a bigger effort if you're getting paid for it. That whole professional ethics thing."

"Not to mention how the legal system views it," I added.

It was a lot to think about—finding a job that didn't make me want to stab my eyes out with a fork, finding a place to live that I could tolerate every day, finding an actual house in the place to live where I could tolerate my neighbors every day, buying furniture and dishes and all those domestic things I'd never quite gotten around to. Basically, I was starting on the ground floor of adulting, and from where I sat, it looked like a whole lot of work.

The biggest problem was having no idea where to start. Gertie was right in that I needed to pin down a location before I worried about a career. Until I knew where I was going to live, I didn't know what careers were viable for the area. If I went the PI route, as Ida Belle suggested, licensing requirements were different by state. More than anything, I wished I could just commit to relocating here and be done with it, but something still held me back. Maybe it was my inability to let go of the only life I'd ever known. Maybe it was my apprehension about my relationship with Carter. Maybe I was afraid that I'd make all these changes and in six months, I'd be bored to death and regretting every one of them.

Bottom line, if I moved to Sinful and it didn't work for me, I'd hurt a lot of people with my exit. Good people. People who mattered. And that was something I really didn't want to do.

"I think it's an interesting idea," I said, "but I want to do some research and see what's required to get a license and what kind of limitations and liability are placed on you once you get that license."

"That's a sound plan." Ida Belle leaned across the table and looked closely at me. "You don't have to make a decision today or tomorrow or even next week. Gertie and I would love to have you here, but only if that's what you want. We don't want you unhappy. That wouldn't work for any of us."

Gertie nodded. "As much as I hate to admit it, Ida Belle's right. We don't want you to leave, but we don't want you miserable, either. You've already got that setup. There's no sense changing your entire life to be right back in it."

I smiled. "You guys are the best, you know it?"

"Of course," Gertie said. She rose from the table and lifted her enormous handbag from the floor. "I've got to go get some bait."

"Going fishing again?" Ida Belle asked.

"Yep," Gertie said. "Still trying for the one that got away."

She tossed some money on the table and headed out of the café at a faster-than-usual clip. Ida Belle watched her go and frowned.

"Something is up with her," Ida Belle said.

"Why? Because she's fishing every day? I thought that was her favorite thing to do—I mean, aside from meddling."

"It is, but this time is different. There's this sense of urgency about it all that she's never had before."

"Maybe it's because her boat was broken for so long, and now that she's finally gotten it fixed, she's making up for lost time."

"Maybe," Ida Belle said, but she didn't sound convinced. Finally, she looked back at me. "So what are you up to today?"

"I don't know," I said, which was the truth and also becoming a real problem.

A week had passed since I'd thrust myself into the middle of a police investigation, and I was ready to climb the walls. Not that I was wanting crime to happen—so far, too many people had died—but maybe a tiny case of petty theft or something. Just enough to challenge the brain and maybe push me into a slow jog through a hedge or onto a roof. Back to the good times.

I sighed. Ida Belle was right. Being a private detective was probably the best job for me. Private security would be a bore. I wasn't interested in ferreting out the secrets of one famous person, and if I ever lost my mind and got interested, there was always TMZ.

Instead, I wanted to know everyone's secrets. Knowing what people had hidden away in the back of their closets made them a lot more interesting than they appeared in everyday life.

Gertie and Ida Belle were prime examples of that. On the surface, they looked like two little old ladies living in a small bayou town. They liked fishing, hunting, knitting, and nosing into other people's business. Completely typical. Except for the part where they had both served in Vietnam as counterintelligence and no one in Sinful aside from me and Carter knew about it. The surface was everything you expected to see, but beneath that murky water were all kinds of things you couldn't have ever imagined.

"You've got to get a hobby or something," Ida Belle said. "I know you can't get a job, but you can't just sit around watching television all day or sleeping in your hammock. I know Carter is occupying some of your time, but his job is more than full time lately, especially with the election results still up in the air."

"Any word on that?" I asked.

Ida Belle and Gertie's nemesis, Celia Arceneaux, had won the recent mayoral election, but her opponent had accused her of vote tampering and asked for an audit, which had been granted. An audit firm was now going over all the votes to determine if Celia was really the mayor of Sinful or if Ida Belle and Gertie's friend Marie was the rightful heir to the swampy throne.

"Not a peep," Ida Belle said. "I talked to Marie yesterday, and she said they have finished the count but that they go through the results two more times until they announce their findings."

"Good God. At the rate they're going, it will be time for a new election before they finish. Or Celia will be dead."

Ida Belle nodded. "We might even have time for Celia to develop a conscience and get nice."

"Evolution for the win."

"Well, if you don't have anything better to do, and you're interested in staying off your couch, I'm going car shopping."

"You're buying a new car? What about the motorcycle?"

"I'm keeping the motorcycle, but there's times when a car is the better option."

"Like when it's raining or humid or summer or when you live in Sinful, Louisiana, and no one can drive for crap?"

"Yeah, some of that."

I rose from my chair and placed some bills on the table. "What the heck. I don't have anything better to do. Plus, I can make sure you get something with a backseat. The middle console of a Corvette is not exactly a comfort zone."

"Could have been worse. Could have been manual transmission."

We headed outside, and I scanned the street for Ida Belle's motorcycle but didn't see it. "Did you walk over?"

"Yeah, too danged hot for leather. And I refuse to be one of those fools who wear a tank top and sandals."

"Good. Then I get to drive. No top on the Jeep, and I can add in AC. Tank tops and sandals are totally optional."

We headed across the road for my Jeep and watched as Gertie exited the General Store, dragging a small ice chest to her car. I hurried over to help her lift it into the backseat and was momentarily surprised at the weight.

"Did you fill this thing with ice?" I asked. "How much can you possibly need for a couple hours of fishing?"

"Ice and bait," Gertie said, "but it's hot out. It melts fast."

She answered without looking at me, never a good sign. Maybe Ida Belle had been right. Maybe Gertie was up to something that she didn't want us to know about. I looked over at Ida Belle, who raised one eyebrow. Unable to help myself, I popped open the lid on the ice chest and peered inside. Four large fish lay on top of the ice. Each one a good eight inches in length.

"This isn't bait," I said. "This is dinner."

Gertie slammed the lid shut. "I said it was bait."

Ida Belle stared at her. "What are you trying to catch—Jaws?"

"Maybe," Gertie said. "Thanks for the help. See you guys later."

She jumped in her car, backed out, and took off down Main Street, leaving Ida Belle and me still standing there, watching her drive off.

"Definitely up to something," Ida Belle said.

I nodded. "I agree, but what in the world is she up to with those fish? That's the strange part. Who uses fish as an alibi?"

"Oldest trick in the book. Guy wants time away from a hovering wife, so he says he's going fishing. Wife approves it because he brings home fish for dinner. But instead of fishing, he buys the fish at the General Store, loads it up with ice, and heads out for a day of whatever."

"But Gertie doesn't have a husband with questions waiting for fish at home."

Ida Belle nodded. "Which makes it even more interesting."

"So you're saying Gertie could be up to anything, anywhere. Why does that sound so scary?"

"Because it contains the words 'Gertie,' 'anything,' and 'anywhere.'"

Chapter Two

We headed to Ida Belle's house to pick up her checkbook and for her to change into her "serious" car-buying clothes, whatever that was supposed to mean. I waited in the Jeep and mulled over why buying a car necessitated a wardrobe change. Ida Belle had been wearing jeans and a button-up yellow fishing shirt earlier. I wouldn't call it serious, but it wasn't as though she was dressed like a hooker or wearing a Halloween costume. Usually, it was Gertie who insisted on an outfit change, so I couldn't wait to see what Ida Belle came out with.

A couple minutes later, she emerged wearing the same jeans and the same shirt, but this time in blue. She climbed into the Jeep and I stared at her. Finally, when she realized I hadn't started the vehicle, she looked over at me.

"Is there a problem?" she asked.

"You changed from a yellow shirt to a blue shirt. The exact same shirt. How is that different?"

"Come on, Fortune, everyone knows yellow isn't a serious color. People see yellow, they think of girls. The last place you want people concentrating on you being a girl is talking to a man selling a car."

I understood the "girl buying a used car" thing—many salesmen didn't have the best reputations for treating women properly—and a senior woman would have a second disadvantage, on paper anyway. Of course, I knew Ida Belle could outthink and definitely outshoot most of the men I'd come across since I'd been in Louisiana, but unless she whipped out a pistol and scared them into a lower price, I wasn't sure that would be useful.

"Where are we going?" I asked.

"Go Fast Auto Sales."

I frowned. It wasn't on the highway between Sinful and New Orleans or I would have seen it. "Where is it?"

"Off the highway a bit. Just start driving. I'll tell you when to turn."

I set off back through downtown and got on the highway that led to New Orleans. "We ought to take a couple days off and head to New Orleans."

"We're off every day. We just need to head to New Orleans one of them."

"True. Then if we can get Gertie to relinquish her fishing pole, maybe we can do it this week."

I'd been to the city several times, but never in a joyous capacity. Mostly, I'd gone there over criminal business, which usually ended in someone shooting at me. I was hoping to see more of the city minus the gunfire.

We'd traveled about ten miles from Sinful when Ida Belle pointed to a road off to the right. It was paved, which was always a good sign. I turned onto it and set off down a narrow road with no shoulder that seemed to lead straight into the marsh. A clump of trees sat in the middle of the marsh grass off to the left and as we drew closer, I realized a large metal building was hidden behind the trees.

"That's the place," Ida Belle said. "Just pull up in front of the shop doors. Hot Rod is expecting us."

"Hot Rod?"

"Hank Comeaux. He can hop up most anything, even push

lawn mowers. People started calling him Hot Rod Hank, then just Hot Rod because it was shorter."

"Why not just Hot?"

"One look at him and you'll retract that question."

I pulled into the driveway and parked in front of a giant set of double doors. A smaller door to the side of the doubles swung open and the skinniest guy I'd ever seen in my life came walking out.

Six foot one. A hundred fifty pounds, including the wrench he's carrying. Muscle content so low, it's a wonder he opened the door. Threat level laughable.

He wore a pair of overalls—probably because he needed the straps to keep pants on—and no other clothing that I could see. No shirt, no shoes, and I wasn't about to think about undergarments. His legs and arms bent all different directions as he walked as though he was a double-jointed praying mantis man.

As he got closer, I refined my assessment. "He looks just like the scarecrow on *The Wizard of Oz*. Only skinnier."

"Nailed it," Ida Belle said. She climbed out of the Jeep and went to shake Hank's hand. "This is my friend Fortune." She pointed at me. "Fortune, this is Hot Rod Hank, southeast Louisiana's answer to Dale Earnhardt's mechanic."

"Nice to meet you," he said, and shook my hand. For a guy with fingers like a corpse, he had a really firm grip. "That's a great vehicle you got there," he said, pointing at my Jeep. "Whenever you're ready to make that thing go like it should, you let me know. I got all kinds of tricks for Jeeps."

Technically, the Jeep was part of the estate that Sandy-Sue Morrow, the woman I was pretending to be, had inherited. While I was hiding out in Sinful, I had use of Sandy-Sue's great-aunt's house and car, but I didn't figure my privileges extended to hopping up the Jeep, although I had to admit more than a little interest in what Hot Rod could do.

"I'll let you know when I'm ready," I said.

He nodded and looked over at Ida Belle. "You ready to see this baby? I think it's going to be perfect for what you want to do."

"Heck yeah!"

I tried to guess what vehicle had them both so excited, but nothing had prepared me for the car that stood in the middle of the shop floor when Hot Rod swung open the big double doors.

"That's a Ferrari," I said.

"You know your cars," he said. "I like a woman that knows cars."

"It has a prancing horse on the front," I said. "What else could it be?"

Hot Rod scowled. "Had a guy last week ask me what model Mustang it was."

Ida Belle shook her head. "That's just wrong. What did you say?"

"Didn't say nothing. Just shot him and kept driving."

I waited for the punch line, but neither Hot Rod nor Ida Belle seemed to find anything wrong with his statement.

"Excuse me," I said, "but you shot the guy for getting the brand of car wrong?"

Hot Rod looked over at Ida Belle, then back at me and grinned. "I'm just funning with ya. Heck, I ain't shooting nobody over a car unless they try to steal it. If people want to walk around stupid then why should I care?"

I walked over to the car and looked at the beautiful lines and shiny red paint. "What model is this?"

"That's a 458 Italia," Hot Rod said. "Normally, I steer clear of Italian women, but Ferrari is my exception. Mind you, they're still just as picky and expensive."

"But they're beautiful," I said. Then reality set in and I looked over at Ida Belle. "You can't buy this car. It's a two-seater. I'd be right back on the center console again."

"While I must admit that it's tempting," Ida Belle said, "this isn't the car we came to look at."

"Oh." I glanced around the shop and realized it contained at least ten other vehicles. "I guess I didn't notice."

Hot Rod nodded. "Happens all the time. The one you came to see is over here."

He set off to the left, and Ida Belle and I trailed behind him. At the rear of the shop, he stopped in front of an old black SUV with too many dents and scratches to count and an unattractive boxy look to it.

"There she is," he said. "Some of the best work I ever did."

I looked back and forth between the two of them, figuring they were pulling my leg again, but they both stood staring at the SUV, grinning like I had at the Ferrari.

"Seriously?" I said. "I don't get it."

"This is K5 Blazer," Ida Belle said. "They're bulletproof."

I leaned closer to the vehicle and studied the door.

"Not for real bulletproof," Ida Belle said. "I was using that as an expression. Not a literal description."

"Oh." I straightened back up, still not understanding. If the vehicle had actually been bulletproof, then that would have been cool, and given our past incidences, it would have come in handy.

"The brush guards and winch are new," Hot Rod said, "but I roughed them up a bit to blend. Put a couple more dents in the sides and the hood as well. There's some scratches, but nothing that goes through the clear coat, so you don't have to worry about rust."

I stared. "You dented and scratched the truck on purpose?"

Ida Belle nodded. "I asked him to. I wanted a sleeper."

I knew what a sleeper was. It was a vehicle that didn't look fast but was fast. On no planet, though, could I picture this big black box tearing up the road.

"I got it up to six hundred," Hot Rod said.

"Six hundred…" He couldn't possibly mean miles per hour.

"Six hundred horsepower," he said.

I pointed at the SUV. "This has six hundred horsepower? How?"

He nodded. "Upgraded engine. Upgrades to the upgraded engine. It's what I do. You want to try it out?"

"Hell yeah!" Ida Belle whooped and opened the passenger-side door, moving the seat up. "Show me what this baby can do. Hurry up and get in, Fortune."

I'll admit, I was considering sitting out the test ride. Something about Hot Rod and Ida Belle's energy level was familiar, and the last time I'd gotten in the middle of it, I'd ended up riding in a Corvette wearing nothing but a garbage bag, then being pulled over by Carter. Granted, I had on clothes now, but there was no telling what kind of event awaited me if I stepped into that vehicle.

Don't be a chicken.

Crap. The chicken thing. It was the one thing I couldn't ignore. If it took my last dying breath, no one in this lifetime would ever have been able to call me a chicken. I said a quick prayer and climbed into the back of the SUV. Ida Belle practically threw the seat back and jumped inside like a circus performer. Hot Rod was grinning like a lottery winner when he climbed into the driver's seat.

I reached up, pretending to scratch my shoulder, and eased the seat belt down, coughing as I clicked it into place. I shouldn't have bothered. A second later, Hot Rod put on his own seat belt and declared, "Better buckle up. You're going to need it."

Ida Belle strapped in, and Hot Rod pressed a button on his key chain. A garage door on the back of the building started to open, and he fired up the SUV. The engine roared to life, and he revved it a couple times. The echo in the metal building was almost deafening.

I should have expected it, but I wasn't ready when Hot Rod put the SUV in reverse and floored it. The truck launched out of the building so fast, I banged my head into the back of Ida Belle's seat. I'd barely managed to get upright again when he put it in gear and floored it again.

The truck raced forward like a roller coaster. I spent a single second admiring the ability of the engine to move this much weight that fast and with linear power distribution, then I switched right back to hoping I'd make it out of the vehicle alive. Hot Rod headed across the yard, but some distance from the driveway. I kept thinking he was going to turn and slide out of the driveway and onto the road, but instead, he ran straight into the ditch, launching all of us out of our seats.

I put my hands up to keep from hitting the top of the vehicle while Ida Belle and Hot Rod whooped it up in the front. They had both officially lost their minds. Or at least, Ida Belle had. Hot Rod might have never had one.

I thought hitting the ditch would slow him down, but it didn't. He launched out of the other side and I swear we were airborne. We crashed into the road and he turned the wheel, sliding us sideways in a layer of mud that covered this section of asphalt. Once I stopped bouncing, I clutched the grab bar, briefly wondering if I had time to get my nine-millimeter out of my waistband and shoot him before he pulled another stunt like that.

"Now for the real power," he said, and I'm certain my eyes

widened all the way to my scalp.

He punched the accelerator and the truck leaped forward, throwing my head back in the seat. It felt as if we were taxiing down a runway in a private jet. Maybe faster. I was pretty sure I was getting younger. The marsh grass on the side of the road blurred into a haze of brown and green, slowly losing color as speed increased even more. I leaned over to look out the front window and I swear it looked like one of those sci-fi movies where the spaceship is just about to go into hyperspace.

I caught a glimpse of a bend in the road ahead of us, then realized it wasn't a bend at all but the entrance to the highway. And we were flying toward it at lightning speed.

"The highway!" I yelled.

Hot Rod glanced back. "Yeah, that's the highway."

I didn't have time to say anything else. It was too late. We were already there.

I started to ask forgiveness for all my sins but then figured this ride had been enough penance to get me through the pearly gates. I tried to close my eyes, but I couldn't stop looking at my impending doom. The concrete of the highway seemed to fill the windshield and then suddenly, Hot Rod yanked the wheel to the left and shot off the road and onto the embankment, launching the vehicle slightly sideways.

He never let off the gas as we made a loop up and down the embankment like a NASCAR racer. When we were back on flat ground, he jammed the brakes and we slammed to a stop. The seat belt tightened so hard it almost knocked the air out of me. Hot Rod and Ida Belle sat there, grinning at each other like idiots, apparently no worse for the wear.

Ida Belle turned around to look at me. "Isn't it great? Now we have a real getaway vehicle and no one will suspect a thing. The brush guards will keep most vehicles from ramming us off the road and the winch will get us out if we get stuck."

Hot Rod shrugged. "I don't know what kind of business you ladies are up to with this car, but whatever it is, the car can handle it." He looked over at Ida Belle. "You want to give it a test drive before you buy?"

"You know it!"

She hopped out and went running around the front of the SUV. Before Hot Rod could get around to the passenger's seat, I crawled over the center console and jumped out of the vehicle.

"You want to ride up front?" Hot Rod asked.

"No," I said. "I want to walk. Assuming I still can."

He looked confused. "It's almost a mile back to the shop."

"I'll be fine. You've got paperwork or whatever to do, right? Don't worry about me."

Ida Belle frowned momentarily, then excitement took over again and she motioned for Hot Rod to get in the SUV. "Hurry up. It's just a mile. She'll be fine. Trust me, she's the deadliest thing out here."

No. I'm not.

I watched Ida Belle tear off down the road in the SUV and couldn't decide which was scarier—her in that vehicle or Gertie with old glasses in her ancient Cadillac. I was considering opting for separate vehicles if we had to go anywhere together. Or maybe a cab. Even a cab in New York was safer.

I set out at a slow jog back to Hot Rod's warehouse of motorized doom, trying to burn off some of the fear I'd collected during the ride. It said a lot about the choices you made in life when jogging actually lowered your heart rate.

By the time I got back to the warehouse, Hot Rod was handing Ida Belle a set of keys and an envelope of papers. Both were still grinning.

"Let me know if you need anything else," Hot Rod said. "I

can get that bulletproof glass you asked about. Just have to order it."

"Go ahead and order it," Ida Belle said, glancing over at me. "You never know with the hunters around here."

Hot Rod nodded. "That's the truth. I was fishing last week and someone put a hole right through the side of my boat. Must have been in the next channel and overshot, but a couple inches to the left and he'd have taken out my knee."

"Did you see him?" I asked, starting to worry a bit since Gertie had been fishing a lot lately. With her refusal to get new glasses and her propensity to be heavily armed at all times, it was more than a passing concern.

"I tried to catch him," Hot Rod said, "but he must have caught on that he overshot when I yelled. He took off out of the channel, and with my boat taking on water, I couldn't keep up. Plus, it was late—sun was already going down so I couldn't see so good."

Ida Belle glanced at me and frowned, and I knew she was wondering the same thing I was. "Did you get a good look at the boat?"

"A decent one. It was a flat-bottom aluminum with an Evinrude motor. The guy didn't look all that big, but he never turned around so that I could see any of his face. Probably too far away to get much of a look anyway, especially with him wearing a ball cap pulled down that low."

Ida Belle's frown disappeared and I took that to mean that Gertie's boat did not have an Evinrude motor and that she was in the clear. It was always a good day when you found out your friend didn't almost accidentally shoot off a man's kneecaps.

"Did you report it to the sheriff?" Ida Belle asked.

"I talked to Carter about it. He came out here and took a look at my boat and said he'd check into it. He's a good guy, but

I'm not sure what he can find. Probably wasn't even someone from around here. That's usually the way it goes."

"Well, we're going to get out of here," Ida Belle said. "Thanks so much for the vehicle. It's going to be perfect."

"I'm glad you like it. I have to admit, I thought hard on keeping it myself." He looked over at me. "When you get ready to hop up that Jeep, you let me know. I can do some serious modifications to a Jeep. Can even get you some artillery racks for the top."

In any other place except the Middle East, I would have found his last statement alarming, but in Sinful, it sounded almost normal. "I'll let you know," I said.

"You want to race home?" Ida Belle asked.

"Are you going to drive in reverse to make it fair?" I asked.

Ida Belle laughed. "Good point."

"You go ahead and do Mach 1 or whatever," I said. "I'll catch up with you in the next dimension."

"I've got a DeLorean on its way from Los Angeles," Hot Rod said. "Check back with me in a couple months. I can get you in that race."

JANA DELEON

Chapter Three

The drive back to downtown Sinful wasn't a long one, but I'm pretty sure Ida Belle made it in about half the time she should have. We left Hot Rod's at the same time, but when I reached the highway, she was already a speck in the distance. I shook my head. I wasn't sure which was more frightening—that Hot Rod thought he could build a *Back to the Future* time-jumping car or Ida Belle's "That's awesome" when he'd delivered that statement.

I didn't see Ida Belle parked anywhere downtown and figured she must have taken her Batmobile directly home to hide it in her garage. I pulled into a spot in front of the General Store, figuring now was as good a time as any to pick up some supplies.

The store was empty, and Walter was in his usual spot behind the counter, doing his usual thing, reading the newspaper. He looked up and smiled when I walked in. "I've been wondering when you'd be in," he said. "I figured you had to be running low on microwave dinners."

Walter was the owner of the store and Carter's uncle. He was also a confirmed bachelor who'd been in love with Ida Belle since the crib. Apparently, if he couldn't marry her, he wasn't interested in anyone else. I had yet to figure out what was keeping Ida Belle from saying yes.

"You know me," I said. "Why learn to cook when the hard part is already done for you?"

Walter made a face. "Because those things taste like crap?"

"Hey, you're the one selling them."

"Who am I to tell people what to eat? You want easy, go for it. You want to eat something worthwhile, you let me know. Grilling isn't that hard. I got a couple of seasoning tricks that will make anything taste great."

"It's too hot to grill, unless you do it at two a.m. Then the mosquitoes will carry you off."

The summer, which had started off hot, had gotten to the hot and miserable stage. With the high humidity, you could break a sweat simply looking out a window, and with no breeze, the mosquitoes had moved from annoying into hostile takeover.

"That's true enough," he said. "That's why I built one of those outdoor kitchens last year and screened it in. Still no AC, but I've got a swamp cooler out there that makes it tolerable long enough to cook. Does a decent job keeping the mosquitoes away as well. Haven't found a screen yet that those suckers can't get through."

"Or material, for that matter. I had one pierce straight through denim the other day. Are you guys feeding them steroids or something?"

"There's a good movie idea. One of those government experiments." He waved a hand at the stool on the other side of the counter. "Have a seat and chat with me for a bit, if you've got the time, that is. It's cool enough in here and I haven't had a chance to talk to you for a while."

While Walter's statement sounded innocuous, what it translated to is 'I haven't had an opportunity to quiz you on Carter lately.'

During the last bit of criminal activity I'd gotten in the middle of, Walter had finally let me know the secret he'd been keeping since the day I arrived—that he knew I wasn't Sandy-Sue

Morrow. He said he had a good guess why I was pretending to be someone I wasn't, but he didn't want to know anything about it. It was smart, really. He was safer not knowing about me.

As of right now, only Ida Belle, Gertie, and Carter knew the truth. Walter had surmised that the reason Carter dumped me was because I hadn't volunteered that truth from the beginning, and the truth about me was something Carter couldn't live with. Walter had gotten it all right. Carter had been more than upset about my lies to him, but at the time, he'd been even more adamant that he didn't want what I did for a living to be part of his life. He'd already had one devastating experience with a woman he loved and the job she did. He wasn't looking for a second.

I couldn't blame him for the way he'd reacted. I was busy questioning everything about the choices I'd made for my life. Who was I to come down on anyone else who did?

I slipped onto the stool and looked Walter directly in the eyes. "Go ahead and get it over with."

"What?" He feigned confusion.

"Don't give me that crap. You want to know about me and Carter."

"Well, I might have been night fishing a couple days ago and noticed him leaving your house at an hour that wouldn't have been considered proper calling time, by Sinful law anyway."

"There's a proper calling time law? Why does that not surprise me?"

Sinful had all sorts of ridiculous laws on the books. I was convinced the founding fathers of the town were drunk the entire time they penned them. Or even worse, they wrote them as a lark and no one had gotten the joke.

"Well, no one really enforces it," Walter said, "but after dark, unmarried women are supposed to have another woman present if they're entertaining a man."

"Seriously? When were these laws written—the Jurassic Era? And did no one stop to think that both women could be there for the same guy?"

Walter took on a pained look. "I'm guessing no one had that in mind at the time."

"Well, to answer your question, I was totally breaking the law the other night. Carter was indeed in my house after dark, and I did not have a single chaperone in sight. Except the cat, but I doubt he counts."

"The cat's male, right?"

I nodded.

"Then he doesn't count."

I stared. "So if he were female, he would have filled the chaperone slot? Please tell me you're joking."

Walter smiled. "How do you think the whole cat lady thing got started, anyway?"

I shook my head. No matter how long I'd been here, things never ceased to boggle my mind. Other countries with completely different languages were less confusing.

"So I guess you guys came to some sort of truce?" Walter asked.

"Some sort of. Carter decided to give some things a pass and I decided to give some things up. We haven't really met in the middle, but we've agreed to try to find it."

"I'm glad to hear it. I think you're good for him, and I guess it's no secret that I like having you around. If I'd ever had a daughter, I would have wanted her to be just like you."

A blush crept up my neck and onto my face. My own father had spent my childhood pawning me off on other people or appearing annoyed at having to spend any time parenting. I was still getting used to people actually wanting me around.

"I would have driven you to drink," I said.

"Certainly, but as I was already a solid beer drinker, you couldn't have done much damage. Probably would have livened things up here, though."

"It *has* been plenty lively since I got here. In fact, I think the town is overdue for a little boredom."

"That's true enough. Things have been quiet the last few days, but I expect feelings will get all up in the air as soon as the election results are announced."

"Any word on that?" I knew what Ida Belle had told me that morning, but sometimes other people had different connections that gave them different inside information.

"One of my regulars has a niece who works in housekeeping at the hotel the auditors are holed up in. She said they started packing up that conference room they're using yesterday."

I perked up. That was good news. Or bad news if the recount favored Celia, but I was betting that it wouldn't. I didn't know how she'd managed to alter the votes, but I had every confidence that she had. Celia would do anything to get an advantage over Ida Belle and Gertie, and as mayor, she had a ton of them.

"That's good," I said. "At least I hope it's good."

"You and me both. If Celia remains mayor, she'll destroy this town out of sheer spite."

"I don't get her. She seems to have a decent life here. I mean, I know her husband was a tool and her daughter was a sleaze and a blackmailer who got herself murdered, but Celia was a miserable piece of work long before any of that, right?"

Walter nodded. "She's been a miserable piece of work since birth. I remember one of the nursery workers at the Catholic church quitting over Celia. In fact, if I remember correctly, her mother had a difficult pregnancy, so it probably goes back to the womb."

"Well, only two things are certain in that case—she's never going to change, and anyone in her sights will always be watching their back."

The door to the storeroom flew open and Carter walked up behind the counter. He looked angry, and I immediately ran through my every waking moment since I'd seen him last, trying to figure out if it was something I'd done. Walter took one look at him and apparently came to the same conclusion that I had.

"You look mad enough to spit," Walter said. "What's up?"

"Alligator poaching," Carter said, each word laced with venom.

Walter frowned. "That's nothing new. We've always had some poaching around here."

"Locals wanting alligator meat for a party, sure," Carter said, "or pros looking to make a quick buck, but this doesn't fit either scenario."

"Why not?" I asked. Poaching was a criminal activity I'd never been exposed to, but if I was even thinking of considering detective work in the South, I figured it was a good idea to understand the crime and the mind-set of the criminal.

"Locals take a single gator or two for whatever event they've got cooking," Walter said. "Usually a decent size, and they skin them in the bayou so the skin can't be found on their property. Unless someone at their party reports them, you usually don't know about it."

"Or unless you're invited to the party," Carter said.

Walter laughed. "Yeah, that wasn't Woody's finest hour, inviting you to a party serving illegally gotten gator."

"Maybe if he hadn't been wearing the head as a hat, I wouldn't have caught on," Carter said.

I grimaced and made a mental note to avoid Woody, especially if he was serving up food or fashion advice. "And what about outsiders doing it for money?" I asked.

"Professionals put out a lot of bait in areas known for large gators," Carter said. "They usually haul out the entire gator because they can sell the skin and the skulls as well as the meat. Unless you find the bait lines and happen to catch them in the act, you won't even know pros passed through your area."

Walter nodded. "And since you know they're here, it's not pros. What did you find?"

"I've found skins of some decent-sized gators, which is nothing out of the ordinary and was probably locals. Then I found a couple dead gators with only their tails missing. The rest of the carcass was tossed back in the bayou."

"That's awful!" I said.

"The strangest part," Carter said, "is that they're all small. None of them were bigger than seven feet long."

"You're right," Walter said. "That doesn't make sense. Did you find bait lines?"

"I found some rope in trees in a couple places, but it wasn't baited. The rope was new, though."

"Maybe they'll be back to bait it," I said. "You should do a stakeout."

"I already did," Carter said. "Sat in the bayou getting eaten up by mosquitoes half of the night. Had two of the bait lines in sight, but there wasn't so much as a stir of air. Then this morning, I got a call about two more small gator carcasses in a completely different location."

"They're moving around," Walter said.

"That's what it looks like," Carter agreed.

"So they're not pros," I said, "but it doesn't sound like locals, either."

"They're definitely not any kind of pro I know about," Carter said. "A couple of the kills were big enough for pros, but the skins were left behind. The rest are too small for pros to bother with. Why kill five small gators when two large ones get you the same thing and run you less risk of getting caught?"

I frowned. He was right. It didn't make much sense. They were taking more chances that they'd be caught by harvesting more gators. So what was the advantage? "How are you going to catch them?" I asked.

Carter shook his head. "I don't know. The only thing I can do is patrol the bayous and have Deputy Breaux do the same. Sheriff Lee is willing, but he falls asleep like clockwork at ten p.m. so he wouldn't be much help."

"What about Wildlife and Fisheries?" Walter asked.

"I've thought about it," Carter said, "but you know how they are. I ask them for help on one issue and they start poking their nose into everything. Next thing you know, I've got a bunch of people fined for having an expired fishing license or not having the right kind of life jacket in their boat. And if they don't pay the fines, I've got to round them up and put them in my jail."

"So it becomes your problem anyway," I said.

"Exactly," Carter said. "Don't get me wrong. If it keeps up, I won't have a choice. Hell, if the state got wind of what was going on now they'd already be pissed I haven't called them in."

"Poachers don't do anything during the day, do they?" I asked.

"Sure," Carter said. "They might bait lines during the day, then come back at night to see if anything is on it. Why do you ask? Have you seen something?"

I shook my head. "But Gertie has been fishing a lot lately, and that got me thinking that with all the people in Sinful who fish regularly, surely someone's seen something."

"Maybe, but there's a lot of bayou to cover," Carter said. "I plan on making rounds to the local fishermen as soon as I leave here, the ones I can find, anyway. I'll probably have to find most tonight, which puts me later getting on the bayou."

Suddenly, I remembered Hot Rod's story about almost being shot. "Hey, I was just at Hot Rod Hank's place with Ida Belle, and he said someone almost shot him when he was out fishing. He said you checked into it."

Carter narrowed his eyes at me. "What were you doing at Hot Rod Hank's place?"

"Ida Belle was buying an SUV from him," I said.

Walter whistled and shook his head. "That's not good."

Carter looked somewhat pained. "Please tell me it wasn't the Blazer."

"Okay," I said. "I won't tell you."

"Jesus H. Christ," Carter said. "That woman will kill someone with that vehicle."

I nodded. "After the test ride, I had the same thought. I'm just not sure whether it will be someone outside the SUV getting run down when it's in warp speed, or someone inside the vehicle having a heart attack. I was close to being in the second category."

"You're not making me feel any better," Carter said.

"Why should you get to feel any better about it than I do?" I asked.

Walter chuckled. "Leave it to Ida Belle to keep things interesting."

"Things are interesting enough lately," Carter said, "without Ida Belle adding to the mix." He looked at me. "But to answer your question, I did talk to Hank and filed a report. And I've already considered that he might have run up against the poacher."

"But why would the poacher shoot at Hank? That would be attracting attention, right? I mean, those guys don't usually kill people, do they?"

"Had a gator on the line and misfired, probably," Carter said. "I went to the spot where Hank was fishing and it was pretty secluded. The poacher wouldn't have seen him from the next channel. The brush was too thick, and there's a good patch of cypress trees as well."

"So you have a description of the man and the boat at least," I said.

"Not much of one," Carter said. "But yeah, it's something. Problem is, that description fits a lot of people around here, and it's not like an Evinrude motor is a unicorn. Lots of people have them."

"But you'll check boats, right?" I asked.

He narrowed his eyes at me. "I'll check boats, and before you get any ideas, I don't need you, Ida Belle, and Gertie helping me out. Poachers don't react well to being caught, and if he thinks you're onto him, he'll shut down operation and I'll never catch him."

I held my hands up in the air. "I wasn't thinking about doing anything. I was just talking. Trying to understand the problem and help if I could. By help, I mean offering an opinion standing here in Walter's store. Not doing anything else."

Carter studied me for several seconds and finally nodded. "Well, I best get going. I've got a lot of people to run down."

He headed out of the store by the front door this time, and I watched as he waved a man down on the street, probably already fishing for clues. I turned back around to face Walter, who was staring at me, his lips quivering.

"What?" I asked.

His smile broke through. "You're a damned good liar, but not good enough to fool me. My nephew isn't quite as experienced, or maybe his feelings for you are clouding his judgment."

"I have no idea what you're talking about."

"All that 'I'm just trying to understand the problem' and 'the only help I'm offering is right here' and so on. That might have gotten you a pass with Carter, but I don't buy a word of it. What are you up to?"

"Nothing. I swear. I mean, nothing to do with the poachers, at least not directly."

"That's an awful lot of backpedaling for someone who's not up to anything."

I sighed. "Fine. I've been considering my options for employment if I were to leave my current position, and Ida Belle suggested I would make a good private detective. So I figured the more I learned about crime, I'd have more to think about when considering a change of profession."

Walter raised his eyebrows and stared at me for several seconds, then nodded. "You've definitely got the nosiness for being a PI. And I'm going to make an assumption that your combat and firearm training is well above average."

"But?"

"Well, I was just wondering why you need to know about alligator poaching. Last time I checked, that wasn't a big thing up in Yankee territory."

I frowned and shuffled my feet. "Maybe I'm thinking about not going back to Yankee territory."

A slow smile spread across Walter's face. "I can tell it makes you uncomfortable so I won't push you. But I will say that I think you'd make a fine addition to Sinful, and I would be really happy if my newest and most interesting friend stayed put."

My chest constricted, and I felt my eyes mist up just a little. I blinked, forcing them back to normal. It was still so hard to process, that people could care so much about me even though they'd only known me for a short amount of time. And in Walter's case, it was even worse.

"You don't even know me," I said.

"I know the important stuff. The rest is just filler. Don't worry about your groceries. I'll pack up some of your usual poison and deliver a week's worth. You're burning daylight. You best get moving."

"Moving where?"

"Into the bayou, of course. You want to catch the poacher, don't you? Prove you can handle small-town crime?"

He grinned, and I hopped off my stool, ran around the counter and gave him a kiss on the cheek, then headed out of the store, waving as I left.

I had a poacher to catch.

Chapter Four

I called Ida Belle and told her I had an emergency and would pick her up in five minutes. She was standing on the sidewalk in front of her house when I pulled up, the *Back to the Future* SUV parked squarely in the middle of her driveway. She was staring at it like a little girl who'd just been given a pony on her birthday.

"If you stare any longer," I said, "you're going to start drooling."

She turned around and grinned before heading over and hopping into my Jeep. "I can't help it. That thing is awesome."

"Well, as much as I hate to add to your extreme speed excitement for the day, we need to make a trip into the bayou on the airboat."

I didn't think it was possible for her to look more excited, but she managed it, which was more than a little scary for me, the passenger. I was decent at driving the airboat, but didn't have near close to Ida Belle's skill, and no way would I ever match her knowledge of the surrounding bayous and channels.

"What's the emergency part?" she asked.

I told her what Carter said about the alligator poacher and how I planned on using this instance to test my ability to be an investigator. "I know we've solved some crimes in the past, but a lot of it feels like we were just rushing into the fire. I need to find out if I can logically pursue an investigation without getting shot at or arrested."

Ida Belle shook her head. "It's going to be hard to manage both of those. Would you settle for one or the other?"

I considered it for a moment. "I'm more accustomed to being shot at, so I guess we should avoid being arrested."

"Given that you're dating a deputy who knows your real identity, and mine and Gertie's, *and* the fact that we're always in the fat middle of his business, I think it might be easier to avoid being shot."

"Even in Sinful?"

"Let me think on it and I'll get back with you. So what's the plan then?"

"I figured we should try to find where the poacher is setting his next group of lines. There's a lot of ground to cover and Carter can't manage it all, not even with Deputy Breaux helping."

Ida Belle nodded. "Plus, it's not a good idea to leave Sheriff Lee to handle Sinful alone for very long, especially when we don't know what Celia might do next."

"She's been suspiciously quiet lately," I agreed. "It makes me nervous."

"It should. So where do you want to start looking?"

"That's where you come in. You know these bayous better than anyone. The poacher is moving around, but he has to have a home base, right?"

"Which in this case would be wherever he launches his boat, so could be a launch or he could live on the bayou."

"Exactly, but I figure he's not going to stray too far from that location because then he increases the risk of being seen. And I'm taking a leap along with Carter that the guy who almost shot Hot Rod could be the poacher, who made a bad shot at a gator."

"That's good thinking," Ida Belle said. "So if we start with" the areas closest to where Hot Rod was fishing, we might find new lines." She pulled out her cell phone. "Let me call Hot Rod and find out where he was exactly."

The call took a bit longer than I would have liked as the conversation segued into Ida Belle's love for the new SUV and potential upgrades and a possibility of even more horsepower, but she finally disconnected.

"Got it," she said. "It's only a fifteen- or twenty-minute ride from your house."

Which translated to 'should be thirty minutes' if anyone but Ida Belle were driving.

I pulled into my driveway. "I assume you're packing."

Ida Belle raised one eyebrow.

"Never mind," I said as we climbed out of the Jeep and headed inside. "Let's grab some binoculars and a couple of bottles of water. Anything else you can think of that we need?"

"Flamethrower? Helicopter? Cannon?" Ida Belle said.

"That sounds like a list Gertie would give me."

"The difference being that she'd attempt to get them." Ida Belle frowned. "Actually, I think she has a flamethrower."

"I don't want to know, and if she's forgotten she has it, for God's sake, don't remind her."

I went into the pantry and grabbed two pairs of binoculars that I kept handy on the shelf while Ida Belle grabbed some waters from the refrigerator. Then we headed out the back door to the airboat. I couldn't help but smile when I looked at the boat, and Ida Belle looked like she's just been crowned queen of England. I wondered if she had to choose between the airboat and her new SUV, which one would win out.

The airboat had been a bit of an issue all the way around. First off, I'd been given the boat by Big and Little Hebert, the local branch of a Louisiana Mafia family, for assisting them with an investigation. My path had crossed the Heberts' several times and in every case, they had surprised me with their commitment to certain values that I hadn't anticipated in mobsters and with their sense of humor concerning some of my more colorful escapades. I know it was a bad idea to be involved at all with the local criminal element, but I couldn't help but like the guys. They were a complete departure from the Hollywood depiction.

Additional problems with the airboat involved my using the boat to interfere with Carter's investigations, Ida Belle's race-boat-driving techniques, and Gertie's adventure on an inflatable alligator that ended badly for Carter and even worse for the alligator. But no matter that drama seemed to cling to it like glue, I wasn't about to get rid of it. I simply liked it too much.

I snagged my life jacket from the storage bench as soon as I got in the boat. Ida Belle rolled her eyes and climbed onto the driver's seat. Normally, the implication of being a sissy was one that brought out the fighter in me, but this was one of the few times people were welcome to think whatever they wanted. No way was I setting foot in the airboat with Ida Belle unless I was wearing a vest. I could swim just fine, but unconscious people usually aren't great at the backstroke. With Ida Belle's driving, the chances of a good crack on the head were higher than I'd like.

I zipped up the vest, then jumped out of the boat, untied it, and shoved it off the bank. I hurried to my seat next to Ida Belle's and my butt had barely made contact with the vinyl before the engine roared to life and the boat leaped forward, pinning me in the seat with no chance of escape. We tore down the bayou, the houses on each side of the bank nothing more than a blur. I could hear the occasional shout, probably from a fisherman unhappy with the wake, but I couldn't actually focus on anyone.

When we reached the bay, she made a hard right. I clutched the arms of the seat and braced my legs against the footrest, trying to maintain my position. Ida Belle whooped as the boat slid sideways on top of the water and doubled down on the throttle as soon as we were going straight again. I began to wonder if a nice boring career down at the DMV was a better long-term plan.

It was a twenty-minute ride to the place where Hot Rod had been fishing. It felt like half that from one perspective and in another way felt like double. Ida Belle killed the engine and pointed at a section of the bank.

"This is about the spot where Hot Rod was fishing," she said. "The shot came from that direction."

I scanned the bank, but it was impossible to see through the trees and brush to the water on the other side. "The shooter had no clear view of Hot Rod."

Ida Belle nodded. "Which makes the theory that he was shooting at something else and missed a good match."

"Let's take a look at the other side."

Ida Belle fired up the boat again, and we pulled around the end of the bank and into the other small body of water. She glided to a spot down the bank a bit and killed the engine again.

"This is probably directly opposite where Hot Rod was," Ida Belle said.

We were about fifteen feet from the bank, and I checked the trees lining the bank. About ten feet down from where we were I spotted a rope dangling from a tree limb that hung over the water. "There," I said.

Ida Belle eased the boat over to the line and grabbed it. "It's fairly new, and this end has been cut."

"Why not take the whole line?"

"He was either in a hurry or thought it wasn't worth the

effort."

"But he wanted the hook, so he cut the end." I frowned. "If he was shooting at a gator and missed, then that means he came back here after almost shooting Hot Rod to collect the gator and the hook."

Ida Belle nodded. "Risky."

"That's what I was thinking."

"Hot Rod said he called it in to Carter that night. The poacher could have run into Carter on a return visit."

"Or an angry Hot Rod," I said. "There's plenty of people in Sinful who would have sat right there on that bank and waited for him to return."

"True. So what're your thoughts? Crazy? Stupid?"

I shook my head. "Maybe stupid crazy?"

"We've got plenty of that around here."

"So how do we narrow them down—the boat engine?"

"It's a place to start. That and alibis for the time of the shooting."

But was it a place to start? I wasn't convinced.

"That can't be the best option," I said. "I can't take every crime that occurs and then eliminate Sinful residents one at a time based on some piece of evidence. We're talking about thousands of people when you take into account all those outside of city limits. By the time we waded through all of them, the criminal would be gone or have covered it up. And what if the poacher isn't local? Then we just spent weeks or months spying on people and creating weird reasons to visit and quiz them. It's not like we can question everyone like the police. No one has to talk to a private investigator."

"Okay, so let's think about it from the opposite side of things to try to narrow it down. What is the type of person who would commit this crime?"

JANA DELEON

I nodded. "That's good. Someone who doesn't have a problem breaking the law, for starters."

"And someone who was more concerned about running away from someone they might have accidentally shot rather than sticking around to make sure they didn't deliver a killing round."

"Remember what Carter said about the size of the gators. The poacher isn't a pro or he'd have the equipment and skill for a bigger catch."

"So stupid crazy. Not a professional. And not worried about shooting someone." Ida Belle looked at me. "Are you thinking what I'm thinking?"

I sighed. "We need to look for the boat at the Swamp Bar."

The Swamp Bar was one of the many banes of my Sinful existence. It was a shack out in the swamp, where the most disreputable of the locals got up to drinking and even more no good. I'd been there a couple of times—never my choice and never for fun—and I'd yet to come away unscathed.

Still, I knew Ida Belle was right. Half of the regulars at the Swamp Bar went by boat, so there was a good chance that if the poacher frequented there, we might luck into finding the boat Hot Rod had seen. Or at least one with the right motor.

It would be a start, anyway.

"Okay," I said. "The need to revisit the Place of My Eternal Embarrassment aside, what now? If we go with my theory that his base of operation is nearby where he sets the lines, then what way do we go now? Are there houses nearby? Or a boat launch?"

"There's a makeshift boat launch about a mile up this bayou. That's the direction he fled in but it was also the direction opposite of Hot Rod, so that doesn't necessarily mean anything."

"Let's check it out."

Ida Belle gave me all of a second and a half to get back in

43

my seat before taking off again. This time, she did a doughnut before shooting out of the channel and back into the main bayou. We were a good hundred feet away before I realized that I hadn't stiffened like I usually did when she launched the boat. Either I was getting used to Ida Belle's driving style or my muscles were fatigued from all the tensing I did earlier. I was sorta hoping it was the latter of the two. It didn't pay to let one's guard down around Ida Belle and a fast vehicle.

We made the drive to the boat launch in a ridiculously short amount of time. It barely felt like she'd gotten up to speed before she was cutting the throttle and turning to the left. I looked at the bank ahead of us and decided that "makeshift" was a super-polite description of the boat launch in front of me.

The remnants of a dilapidated dock jutted out from the bank, a few lonely, warped planks of wood clinging to the pylons. A small clearing of dirt that would hold maybe two trucks and boat trailers max was just beyond what was left of the dock.

"Where is the launch?" I asked.

"You're looking at it," Ida Belle said.

"There's no ramp here." I waved my hands at the grassy embankment.

"That marsh grass is the launch. Don't let how it's standing fool you. It springs right back up after being pressed down. A long time ago there was cement, but it broke apart years ago. This used to be Old Man Johnson's camp. He's the one who put the boat launch in."

"Why didn't he keep it up?"

"When I said 'old,' it wasn't one of those colorful Southern sort of endearments. Old Man Johnson was old as Christ when I was still a kid. He died decades ago, and his wife had gone years before that. He had a couple kids who inherited this, I guess, but no one ever came out here. Katrina took out what was left of the camp. But the slope for the launch is still there. It won't hold anything heavy, but you could launch a boat the size Hot Rod saw here."

"Where does the road come out?"

"It's an old dirt road, best I can remember. There's a couple turns onto other dirt roads, but the whole mess eventually dumps you onto the access road for the highway."

"Well, enough people are using it to keep the grass from growing over the parking area. If the poacher is using this place, that's another risk. I mean, he could throw a tarp over the gators, but wouldn't that raise a few eyebrows?"

"Exactly the opposite, actually. Everyone would know he had something illegal under the tarp, and they'd intentionally avoid looking at him. You let on that you know someone's up to poaching, and you might find yourself under the tarp with whatever else they have."

"Good point."

"But it does mean someone else might have seen something. Once news of the poacher starts leaking out, someone who wouldn't stick his neck out here at the launch might have a word with Carter."

"So it's still riskier to use a place frequented by others."

"Yeah. It's more likely he has a camp on the bayou. Tossed the tails right up on his pier and filleted them in the privacy of his own home, probably drinking a beer and watching the sports channel."

I nodded. "Let's go farther down the bayou and see if there are any camps visible from the main bayou."

"You got it."

Ida Belle set off down the bayou, but this time at a much slower clip so that we could see down the channels and inlets that branched off the main source. I peered down one after the other but with the dense brush, it was impossible to know what else might lie down them.

"We'd have to go down every single one of these to know what was there," I said. "It would take forever."

"Maybe not," Ida Belle said. "I have an idea, but I need to pick up some equipment."

"What idea?"

She waved a hand in dismissal. "I'm not sure it will work so I don't want to get your hopes up. Let me check on it and I'll let you know tomorrow."

I was about to press for more information when a boat shot out of one of the channels right in front of us, and it was a miracle that we didn't broadside it. Ida Belle yelled at the other boater, who spun his boat around and glared at us as if the entire event had been our fault. I was just about to give him a far bigger piece of my mind than Ida Belle had when I saw the Wildlife and Fisheries stamp on the side of his boat.

Midthirties. Five feet eight. A hundred ninety pounds. Okay muscle content. Crappy attitude.

The last one was a guess but as soon as he opened his mouth, he verified it.

"You need to watch where you're going," he said, scowling at the two of us.

"I think you need to take your own advice," Ida Belle shot back, clearly unimpressed by his driving and his position with the state. "Last time I checked, the person entering the larger body of water should yield."

"I don't need you telling me how to navigate these waters," he said.

"You need someone telling you," Ida Belle said. "Because clearly, you're doing it wrong."

He narrowed his eyes at us. "What are you doing here anyway? You've got no fishing equipment, and don't tell me you're working on your tan."

"Bird-watching," Ida Belle said, and held up the binoculars hanging around her neck.

"Sure," he said. "Then you won't mind if I search your boat, will you?"

"Search away," Ida Belle said.

I looked over at her and she gave me a tiny shake of her head. Angry Man boarded the airboat and lifted the cover off the bench seat and peered inside. It didn't take long to make his way through two life jackets and an ice chest with four bottled waters in it. He slammed the cover back down and stomped back onto his own boat.

"Watch where you're going from now on," he said, "and I suggest you stick to the main waterways. You're likely to run into trouble on the bayous."

He started his boat and took off down the bayou. We both sat staring after him.

"What the hell was that?" I asked.

Ida Belle frowned. "He thought we might be poachers."

Then it hit me. "Holy crap! That means Wildlife and Fisheries knows about the problem. Carter is not going to be happy when he hears about this."

"Look on the bright side," Ida Belle said. "At least this time when Carter's angry, we didn't do it."

After our run-in with angry Wildlife and Fisheries man, we decided boating in the opposite direction was probably the best plan. He might not think we were poachers any longer, but he hadn't bought that bird-watching thing, either. We covered a huge amount of ground, but I'd bet anything it didn't even put a dent in the scope of water surrounding Sinful. In three hours of riding, we hadn't seen any other signs of bait lines. We had just turned down yet another channel when we spotted Gertie ahead of us, but she wasn't fishing.

She was leaned over the side of her boat, peering into the water like she was summoning a mermaid. When she heard our boat, she jerked up and grabbed her fishing rod. A couple seconds later, we pulled up beside her.

"What the heck are you looking at?" Ida Belle asked.

Gertie looked slightly flustered, and she hesitated a second before answering. "I was checking the water for clarity. The fishing is better when the water's clear."

Ida Belle raised one eyebrow. "The water in Sinful hasn't been clear since God created Earth. Even my bathwater is sketchy."

"Sometimes it's murkier than others," Gertie insisted.

I could tell Gertie was hiding something and that Ida Belle knew she was lying, but whatever Gertie was up to, it was clear she wasn't ready to share it with the two of us. Since she was usually the first to blab about everything, my curiosity was sky high, but I also knew her well enough to know that we wouldn't get it out of her until she was ready to tell.

"What are you two doing out here?" Gertie asked.

"Looking for a poacher," I said.

"What poacher?" Gertie asked.

I filled her in on everything we knew about the poacher and on our day of checking channels for evidence. "You haven't noticed anything strange while you were fishing, have you?" I asked.

"Slim Thibodeaux went by wearing a Batman costume. His dog was dressed as Wonder Woman. The dog's male, so…"

Ida Belle waved a hand in dismissal. "He's had those costumes for years. She meant anything outside of the ordinary."

Gertie scrunched her brow in concentration and finally shook her head. "Maisey Jackson was boating naked again, but that's nothing new. I can't think of anything else."

"Thank God," I muttered. Those two were bad enough.

"Well," Ida Belle said, "looks like we're on to plan B."

"What's plan B?" Gertie asked.

"A trip to the Swamp Bar to look for the boat that Hot Rod saw," Ida Belle said.

Gertie's eyes widened, and she clapped her hands. "I have some ideas about disguises."

"I'm not going to be slutty again," I said. "I'm always slutty."

"It is the Swamp Bar," Ida Belle said. "If you dress like the church lady, you're not going to blend."

"Why can't I just wear jeans and a T-shirt?"

"Because too many people know who you are now," Gertie said. "You're a sight better-looking than the average Sinful fare. When are we going?"

"I'm having dinner with Carter tonight," I said. "If I cancel, he'll get suspicious, so it's either tomorrow or we have to go late tonight."

Gertie shook her head in dismay. "You're having dinner with the hottest guy in Sinful and you expect to spend the rest of the night alone. Where did I go wrong with you?"

"I'm pretty sure she was that way before you got a hold of her," Ida Belle said.

"You would know," Gertie said, "leaving Walter hanging for sixty years. How do you know she's not learning that trick from you?"

"How did this become about me?" Ida Belle said.

49

"I don't like rushing things," I interrupted before they got too deep.

"You're practically going in reverse," Gertie said. "If you get any slower, he's going to need Viagra."

"I'm not worried," I said. "He's got good medical insurance."

"So tomorrow night," Ida Belle said. "That's better anyway. We need to come up with a list of Sinful residents. I don't know why I didn't think of this before, but it's probably something we should have handy and keep updated."

"How are you going to get a list of thousands of people?" I asked.

"I'll start with the phone book and church registry and go from there. The Sinful Ladies can help. I'll tell them it's about the election—that I'm looking for a list to work in case this thing goes to a revote."

I had to admit, I wouldn't mind having a database of Sinful locals, especially if other information were noted. "I don't suppose you could add information like sex and age?"

"Sex is easy enough," Ida Belle said. "We'd be guessing at age. A lot of the older generation lie about that kind of thing and some have simply forgotten, but we can make an educated assessment in most cases."

"That would be awesome," I said, and looked up at the sky. "I need to get home. I got roped into providing dinner."

"You're cooking?" Gertie cast a nervous glance at Ida Belle.

"God no," I said. "Ally's bringing over casserole, sides, and dessert, but I have to get instructions on how to heat everything."

"Smart," Gertie said. "Are we going to the Swamp Bar by car or boat?"

"Car," Ida Belle said. "We're looking for a guy in a boat. No use giving him a way to chase us."

"Why would he chase us?" I asked. "Chasing isn't part of the plan."

Gertie shook her head. "It never is."

Chapter Five

My friend Ally was sitting in a lawn chair in my backyard when Ida Belle roared halfway up the bank in the airboat. The boat jolted as it came in contact with land, and I clung to the armrests so hard I thought my fingers would break, barely managing to avoid pitching out of the seat. Ida Belle, as usual, looked as if we'd drifted up following a slow row.

"That does it," I said. "I'm getting seat belts for this thing."

"A racing harness might be a better idea," Ally chimed in.

Ida Belle waved a hand in dismissal. "Bunch of pansies."

"Call me Violet, then," Ally said. "You couldn't pay me to get in that thing."

I hopped out of the boat and onto the bank, Ida Belle traipsing behind me.

"You heard anything from your aunt?" Ida Belle asked Ally.

Ally had the unfortunate luck of being related to Celia Arceneaux. They'd had a falling-out recently—several, actually—and Celia had taken to no longer speaking to Ally for a while. Unfortunately, when Celia had realized Ally preferred the silent treatment, she'd started talking again, and at length.

Ally rolled her eyes and her expression was that of a long-suffering spouse. "I've heard *everything* from Aunt Celia. I keep thinking she'll die of asphyxiation because she doesn't stop long enough to take a breath, but so far, no luck."

"Demons don't need to breathe," Ida Belle said. "But let

me rephrase the question to something useful. Has she said anything relevant?"

Ally shook her head. "Mostly a lot of ranting about the election audit and why it's taking so long. And that if she's not the clear winner then the audit was rigged. I asked her how that could be, and you'll love her answer—she says Fortune is doing 'favors' for the auditors to get them on Marie's side."

I threw my hands in the air. "Why am I always the slut? I'm always the slut."

"Hot women who get the guys are always the slut," Ally said.

"You're never the slut," I argued.

"That's because Carter is the only decent catch in town and he's after you," Ally said. "If he were after me, I'd be the slut."

"Well, maybe this town needs to import some more eligible men," I said.

"Preach!" Ally said.

"This whole slut thing is getting old," I groused.

Ida Belle nodded. "Especially when you're not even getting any. Doesn't seem fair, really."

"That's beside the point," I said.

"Not really," Ally said. "If everyone's talking anyway, you might as well have some fun. If you don't get lucky after the dinner I prepared, then there's no hope for you."

"What if I don't want to get lucky?" I asked.

"Everyone wants to get lucky," Ally said. "They just don't want to admit it."

"All this talk of getting lucky reminds me that I need to wax my new love," Ida Belle said. "Talk to you tomorrow."

Ally's eyes widened and she stared after Ida Belle as she walked away. "Ida Belle has a new love? Tell! And elaborate on the wax part."

"Don't get excited. It's an SUV. I'll admit, it got my heart racing, but that was mostly fear."

"She's been shopping with Hot Rod. That's scary, but it does make me feel better about the waxing part."

I nodded and we headed for the house. "The town should probably send out a warning, or sound that hurricane siren thingie. Let everyone know to be on guard."

Ally laughed. "It can't be that bad."

"I got halfway through the test ride and walked back. Seriously, that whole *Star Wars* warp speed stuff is nothing."

"Well then, we better get inside and go over your dinner preparations," she said as we headed up the back steps and into the kitchen. "This could be your last night on earth if you plan on riding with Ida Belle again."

"I know you think you're joking, but I wouldn't place a bet on it or anything." I checked out the two huge pots and covered baking dish on the stove and said a silent prayer that nothing required me to actually know anything besides how to turn on the oven. "So what does my last meal consist of?"

Ally clapped her hands and grinned. "You're going to love this. Carter was at the café for a late lunch the other day and he was asking when Francine was going to make crawfish étouffée again. She doesn't do it often because it's such a process in a small kitchen, but it's Carter's favorite."

"You made étouffée? Seriously, that is above and beyond the friendship requirement."

"You let me live with you while my kitchen was being rebuilt."

"And you fed me goodies every single day. It's not like I was suffering." I lifted the lid off the pot and the smell of crawfish, spice, onions, and a whole host of other wonderful things wafted up. "I might cry. Oh my God, that smells incredible."

Ally blushed, as she always did when I complimented her cooking, but I could tell she was pleased. "I'm glad you're happy with the choice. I started not to...I know you said you guys' breakup was mutual and all, and I'm not asking you to go into details, but I still say Carter was a fool to let you get away, even if it wasn't for long. And well, I wasn't completely convinced he deserved étouffée."

"I'm not the easiest person to get along with."

"Please. I lived with you and trust me, you're very low-maintenance and completely laid-back, unless you're sleeping. If you and Carter ever progress to spending the night together, you probably want to warn him not to startle you out of sleep."

On a couple of occasions while she was staying with me, Ally had found out just how quickly I could vault from the bed and level a gun. Fortunately for me, she'd taken my "single woman living alone in the big city" explanation and laughed it off.

"I'm sure Carter could disarm me, if it came down to that," I said.

I wasn't the least bit sure of that at all, but it sounded like the sort of thing a librarian would say, and as far as Ally knew, that's exactly what I was.

"You're also forgetting all the grief I've caused him by getting in the middle of his investigations along with the meddling twosome," I said.

"And ended up catching murderers. He ought to be thanking you. Besides, Ida Belle and Gertie have been nosing into everything in this town since they could walk, and Carter knows good and well that won't change until they both pass. Heck, even then, I wouldn't put it past them to come back and haunt us all."

"I could see that."

Ally checked her watch and sighed. "I have to run. I agreed to bake a hundred cookies for Aunt Celia and one of her church things."

"Why on earth would you agree to do something for Celia?"

"Because it was the easiest way to get her to shut up and go away."

I nodded. "So what are my instructions?"

Ally pulled a folded paper from her pocket. "I wrote it all down, just to make sure. I mean, I'm not saying you wouldn't remember, but…"

I took the paper and scanned the notes. "Written is definitely better. And this looks simple enough. Turn a knob, set a timer. What can go wrong?"

"I'd really rather you didn't put questions like that out in the universe, especially the universe surrounding Sinful."

"Good point. I'll amend to 'I think I can handle this.' If I get confused, I'll call. If it's too late to call, I have a fire extinguisher in the pantry."

"That's all a girl can ask." She gave me a quick hug. "Good luck. I'll give you a call tomorrow to see how it went. And please, I'm begging you—"

"Don't do anything you wouldn't do?"

"No. Please do *everything* I don't have the opportunity to do."

The bread had just gotten to that perfect crusty point when I heard my front door open and close. Seconds later, Carter walked into the kitchen, sniffing the air.

"When I said you were responsible for dinner," Carter said as he stepped up to the stove, "I thought it was a gamble and I might get one of those awful frozen things, but it smells like you called in reinforcements."

I lifted the lid on the pot of étouffée and allowed him to take a whiff. "How do you know I didn't make this myself?"

He raised one eyebrow.

"Never mind."

"Ally, I presume?"

I nodded. "No use doing things halfway."

"I agree," Carter said, and produced a bottle of wine. "I brought this."

He leaned in. "And this," he said as he lowered his lips to mine.

I relaxed into his kiss and moved closer as he wrapped one arm around my waist. I slipped my arms around him, and he deepened the kiss. I couldn't believe how much I'd missed him while we were separated, and I still marveled at the way my body responded every time he touched me.

On a completely other level, it scared the crap out of me.

I was finally getting used to having real friends, but just the thought of a romantic relationship that had the potential of a future was enough to send me into panic. I'd overthrown entire governments without my blood pressure going up even a tick, but having this man want me was more than my inexperienced mind could process. My heart handled it by pumping harder and making me slightly dizzy. We needed to chat, me and my heart, but I had a feeling my mind was going to lose any argument it put forward.

He broke off the kiss and smiled. "We better have dinner before it gets cold, and where this is headed would guarantee a cold meal."

I smiled and grabbed some bowls from the cabinet next to the sink. I knew he was lying...in a way. Carter would have been happy to continue on the path he'd started and microwave the dinner afterward, but he must have sensed my hesitation. His backing off made me even more attracted to him. Was there anything wrong with the man? I mean, besides his somewhat short temper and his apparent poor judgment when it came to women?

"Ida Belle and I took the airboat out for a spin today," I said as we took our bowls of food to the kitchen table and sat down.

"Any particular reason why?"

I shook my head. "Just wanted to get some sunshine without sweating to death. I get stir-crazy sitting in the house all day."

He nodded. "We've reached that time of the year where most people with the option stay inside and hibernate until September."

"Sane people, you mean? Gertie went fishing."

He grinned. "And you went for an airboat ride with Ida Belle. Even if it was seventy degrees and clear skies, that doesn't put you on the sane list."

"True. Anyway, we almost got run over by a dude from Wildlife and Fisheries." I told Carter about the incident and his grin vanished, replaced with a frown.

"You're sure he was from the state?"

"It was on the side of the boat."

"Dark brown hair? Short man's syndrome?"

"That's definitely the guy. Was Ida Belle right? Did he really think we were poachers?"

"Maybe, but we've crossed paths a time or two. More likely he was pissed for being called out for his crap driving and was looking for another reason to cite you."

"I've never seen a game warden around before, just random

like that, but then I don't spend all my time on the water. Is it normal?"

Carter slowly shook his head. "The state doesn't ever show up just because."

"You think they got wind of the poacher?"

"Given that no one contacted me that they'd have a warden in the area, probably."

"And now they're hacked off that they didn't hear it from you."

"Or they think I could be the poacher."

"What? Seriously?"

He nodded. "It wouldn't be the first or last time that the local law enforcement was the head of a poaching ring. Still, I'm hoping they're just angry over lack of notification. If I were going to poach, it wouldn't be small gators. I would hope even the state knows that much. Where did you run into him?"

I described the location, and he narrowed his eyes at me. "That's close to where Hank was when he got shot at. Why would you go all the way down those narrow bayous when there's a great big lake where you can get all the wind in your face that you need?"

"We were looking for Gertie," I said, throwing out the first thing I could think of that might make sense. "Ida Belle said she liked to fish in that area. I guess a lot of people do."

I was totally firing in the dark. I had no idea if people liked fishing in that area. I only knew Hank and Gertie claimed to fish there and two hardly made it a fact, but I must have hit a bull's-eye because Carter's eyes returned to normal size.

"It's a fairly popular area for fishing," he finally admitted.

"Then it doesn't seem like it would be a very good one for poaching if a lot of people are around."

"That's just it. They're not around right now. Only a

handful of amateur fishermen bother this time of year. The rest eat frozen dinners and complain a lot about summer."

"Oh! The heat." Suddenly, it all made a lot more sense. If the fishing was good, then that meant alligators had plenty to eat, which meant more alligators. And since the fishermen were mostly inside enjoying a cold beer and AC, then the poacher didn't have as much risk now as he would in cooler weather.

I held up my spoon, a thought coming to me. "Hey, Gertie said she saw someone boating naked. That would be cooler, right?"

Carter grimaced. "And illegal and definitely not how you'd want to be outfitted to pull an alligator into a boat."

"Yeah, probably not."

He raised his eyebrows.

"Okay, definitely not. But you can't blame me for suggesting it. This place isn't exactly normal."

"And you're the authority on what normal living looks like?"

"Touché."

"Can we move on to more pleasant topics than Maisey Jackson's frightening boating habits?"

I couldn't help the grin.

Carter had just finished the last bite of dessert when someone knocked on my door. I frowned. Ida Belle, Gertie, and Ally knew I had a date and wouldn't interrupt unless it was an emergency. And if it was an emergency, they would have barged in.

Or maybe not.

I sighed. If they thought I was getting lucky, they might resort to actually knocking.

"You expecting anyone?" Carter asked.

"Who would I be expecting? My friends know I'm having dinner with you, and no one else wants to see me."

I headed to the front door and was surprised to see Deputy Breaux standing there. Then I panicked.

"Is someone hurt? Did Ida Belle wreck that devil SUV of hers? Did Gertie blow something up? Did either one of them shoot Celia?"

Deputy Breaux held his hands up. "None of those things happened, and God willing, they won't. Well, except maybe the last one, but you never heard me say that. I heard Carter was here. I need to talk to him."

I flung open the screen door. "Then why didn't you say so? He's in the kitchen."

Deputy Breaux followed me back to the kitchen where Carter was putting the dishes in the dishwasher. He looked up when we entered the room and frowned when he saw the deputy.

"I'm sorry to interrupt your dinner," Deputy Breaux said, "but we've got a problem. Shrimpers found two gator skins in their nets."

"What size?"

"Small. They'd guess about six feet or so."

"Where did the shrimpers find them?"

"They were pushing in the lake."

Carter blew out a breath. "Which means the skins could have emptied there from a hundred different bayous."

"They were on the south side," Deputy Breaux said, "and the skins still had a bit of meat on them. They hadn't been in the water too long or they'd have been stripped bare."

Carter looked out the kitchen window. "It's not even dark yet. What kind of fool skins an illegally killed alligator on the bayou and in broad daylight?"

Deputy Breaux shook his head. "I guess if his boat was deep enough, people might not be able to see, but it's a big risk."

"Yeah, even bigger since I've found out that Wildlife and Fisheries is cruising the bayous here."

Deputy Breaux's eyes widened. "You're sure?"

"He almost ran Ida Belle and me over this afternoon," I said. "Real piece of work, that guy."

"But how did they find out?" Deputy Breaux asked. "We didn't even know until a couple days ago. Why would someone report it to the state without telling us?"

"Because they're friends with Celia?" I suggested.

"We can't blame everything bad that happens in Sinful on Celia," Carter said.

"Why not?"

Deputy Breaux and I sounded off in unison.

"Because as much aggravation as the woman is responsible for, she doesn't know everything. When was the last time you saw Celia on a boat, or even near water? Or talking to a shrimper or a fisherman, or quite frankly, anyone she considered beneath her, which is most of the town?"

"That's true," I said. "Besides, if Celia had called the state, she'd have been down at the sheriff's department gloating about it."

Carter sighed. "I guess I better take a look at the lake before it gets dark."

"Scooter's rebuilding the carburetor on the department boat. He said it will be at least another two hours before he's done."

"In two hours, it will be dark," Carter said. He looked out my kitchen window, then back at me. "I don't suppose you'd let me borrow your boat."

"Sure," I said, "as long as I go with you."

He shook his head. "I can't authorize that. It could be dangerous."

"It could be more dangerous taking my boat and leaving me here."

Deputy Breaux looked completely confused, but I knew my statement wasn't lost on Carter.

"If I don't go with you," I said, "all those leftovers might evaporate into the night. That would be a shame. All that étouffée and dessert gone just like that."

Carter looked pained. "You wouldn't."

I smiled. "You know better."

He sighed. "Fine. But you're wearing a life jacket, and you don't move out of the boat unless I say so."

I held up one hand. "I will not exit the boat unless we're back on shore or it's on fire."

"Could you not say that so loud?"

Chapter Six

Carter was a much more conservative driver than Ida Belle, but then I was pretty sure Dale Earnhardt Jr. was a more conservative driver than Ida Belle. When we reached the place in the lake where the shrimpers pulled up the skins, Carter killed the engine and scanned the area. Finally, he threw a stick in the water and watched it move with the tide.

"I guess that means the skins came from a channel to the south of us?" I asked.

"Yeah, but that leaves a lot of ground to cover."

I pointed off to our left. "I think Ida Belle and I were somewhere over there, but I'm not sure exactly. They all look alike to me."

"Unless you spend a lot of time out here, it's easy to get lost. Between Gertie fishing, you and Ida Belle tearing up the bayou in the boat, and Wildlife and Fisheries hanging around, my guess is the poacher wasn't anywhere near you guys."

"Soooooooooo, to the right?"

He started the boat and swung it to the right, picking one of the medium-sized channels to cruise. We were about halfway down the channel when I thought to ask, "What are we looking for exactly?"

"Bait line, floating skins, or other parts that are buoyant."

We cruised that channel until it became too narrow for a regular boat to navigate without potential problems and turned around. Carter repeated the process with five more channels. When we were about to exit one of the channels, I saw something dangling from a branch on a cypress tree next to the bank on our right.

"I think I see something there," I said, and pointed.

Carter slowed the boat to a crawl and approached the cypress tree. The sun was going down on the other side of the tree, so it cast a dark shadow onto the bayou.

"Where?" Carter asked as we pulled underneath the tree and he cut the engine.

I scanned the tree, looking for the rope, but couldn't find it. "Maybe I was mistaken," I said. "Wait! There it is."

I pointed to the black rope hanging directly above us, and that's when I realized the rope was moving. Carter reached for the ignition, but it was too late. The snake dropped out of the tree and right onto me. I yelled and grabbed the snake from my shoulders, flinging it in the air. Not even a second later, I leaped out of my seat, pulled my nine, and shot it.

As the snake split into two pieces and dropped, two men rounded the corner in a small fishing boat. The snake parts fell into their boat and they both jumped up, pulling out guns and firing. Carter dove off his seat and we both hit the deck, covering our heads with our hands and praying that they ran out of bullets soon.

Finally, the gunfire stopped and all that was left was yelling.

We peered up over the edge of the airboat and saw the two men grabbing fishing poles and tackle boxes as their boat sank lower in the water.

Carter jumped up and started the boat, then rushed it forward next to the sinking fishermen. I managed to stuff my pistol into my waistband and get back into my seat as the two men jumped into my boat, hands full of fishing tackle. We all watched as the boat gave its final glurg and disappeared below the surface.

"What the hell were you doing shooting the boat?" the first man yelled.

The second man glared. "I didn't shoot the boat. You're the lousy shot. I got the snakes."

"Gentlemen," Carter interrupted. "Your insurance company can sort out who shot the boat, assuming, of course, that's the story you give them."

The first man must have been the boat owner, because he looked at Carter as if he'd lost his mind. "Hell no, I ain't telling insurance how it happened. You think they're going to believe we were attacked by flying snakes? I've lived in these bayous fifty-six years and never heard of such a thing. Wouldn't believe it now if I hadn't seen it."

"I'm sure you're right," Carter said. "Maybe you can say you hit something and started taking on water too fast to recover. Probably best if you claim you were out in the middle of the lake somewhere. Then they won't send a diver for it."

The boat owner frowned, then nodded. "That's good. That's really good. But ain't you got to file a report or something?"

Carter shook his head. "As far as I'm concerned, I didn't see a thing. As far as you're concerned, I was never here."

We dropped the men off at the sheriff's department dock and headed back to my house. Carter pulled the boat onto the bank, and I hopped out and tied it off to a post in my yard. He climbed out and stared at me for several seconds, not saying a word.

"What?" I asked. "Don't give me that look. I kept my promise. I didn't get out of the boat."

"No, John Wayne. But you managed to indirectly sink a

boat."

"If you want to run around with snakes on your head, feel free, but I have personal space issues."

His lips quivered for a moment, then he finally laughed. "Did you have to shoot it?"

"If I'd just thrown it, it probably still would have landed in their boat anyway. The only difference is it would have been alive."

"For about a second. Then those two would have blasted it into a million pieces, right along with their boat."

I held both hands up. "See. Same ending."

He shook his head. "Why didn't you tell me you were carrying?"

"You really want to know every time I strap on a gun?"

"Look, I'm not even going to try to tell you not to. I get why you do it, but it would make me feel better if I knew there was a chance you were going to open fire on defenseless creatures."

"How about you assume that unless I'm naked, I'm carrying."

He smiled. "Sounds like a good excuse to get you naked."

I was dreaming of a bowl of crawfish étouffée when my phone rang. I grabbed it off the nightstand and jumped out of bed and into a firing positing, the phone pointed at the bedroom door. I sighed and lowered my arm, rotating it at the shoulder. I was getting stiff from lack of exercise. I needed to work out more, and not in an aerobic-bad-guys-chasing-me sort of way. Definitely not in a snake-dropping-from-above sort of way.

I realized I'd never answered the phone and saw I'd missed a call from Gertie. A second later, the phone signaled an incoming text.

Emergency meeting at my house asap.

She'd sent it to both Ida Belle and me.

What the heck now?

An emergency call from Gertie could mean anything from losing the television remote to an explosion or possibly even a body. It was a troubling call on many levels, but mostly because I was never quite sure what kind of supplies to bring—tarp, shovel, fire extinguisher, spare remote—the list was endless.

I threw on clothes and hurried downstairs, grabbing my Jeep keys and a soda on the way out of the house. I'd just go assess the situation, then if there was time, have some breakfast, then head home for whatever supplies were needed to handle Gertie's latest situation.

Ida Belle's age-reducing SUV wasn't at Gertie's when I got there, so I pulled into the driveway and headed up to the house. The front door was unlocked, so I pushed it open and called out, but all I heard was the oven timer. I headed back to the kitchen, but it was empty except for whatever was baking. I pulled open the oven and took a whiff, then covered my mouth and nose with one hand and slammed the oven shut with the other. Whatever Gertie had in there, I hoped she wasn't serving it up for breakfast. It smelled like rotting fish.

My appetite completely gone, I headed to the staircase and yelled up for Gertie, figuring she was probably in her bedroom. When no answer was forthcoming, I started up the stairs, getting a bit aggravated that Gertie had disappeared after her emergency summons. I was halfway up the stairs when I heard a noise below me. It sounded like something bumping against a wall.

When Gertie was injured, she sometimes took up residence in the downstairs guest room to keep from going up and down the stairs. She wasn't injured when Ida Belle and I had left her yesterday, but there was a lot of time in between and it didn't take too much of it for Gertie to get into trouble. What if she'd fallen somewhere? But then why didn't she call 911 or say she'd fallen in her text?

I hurried back down the stairs and down the hallway to the guest room, but the bed looked the way it always did when it was made up for company, every pillow in place. Then another bump rattled the wall behind me and I whirled around and stared at the bathroom door, which was closed. That door was never closed. There wasn't an AC vent in the bathroom, so unless it was in use by a visitor, Gertie insisted the door be kept open for circulation. I was also fairly certain she wouldn't close the door to use the bathroom if she was alone in her own house. Nor would she have left the front door unlocked if she was sequestered in the bathroom.

So who was in there?

I stepped over and put my ear up to the door, but all I heard was a couple of knocks, like someone was bumping into the toilet or sink. I knocked on the door.

"Gertie? Are you in there?"

The bumping stopped. I knocked again.

"Are you injured? You've got three seconds to respond, then I'm opening the door. One, two, three."

I pushed the door open and immediately realized my mistake. This was one of those times when I should have inched it opened and taken a peek, because all I'd done was provide a wide exit for the creature inside.

The alligator took one look at me and launched out of the bathtub of water, hissing. I slammed the door shut and took off out of the bedroom as if it were about to explode…and it sorta did.

I heard the alligator crash through the bathroom door as I

rounded the corner from the hallway and into the kitchen. The sound of his claws on the hardwood floors was way to close for comfort, and when I glanced back, I saw the beast dashing out of the hallway, his legs extended, and moving faster than I thought that much length should be able to manage.

I didn't even bother pausing to open the screen door. I just ran right through it, leaped off the porch, and landed in the backyard, sprinting for the nearest tree that would hold my weight for the next hour to fifty years—however long it took for the rescue squad to get here. I could hear the alligator running behind me, his body creating a swishing sound on the grass. My legs protested briefly at the sprint with no warm-up, but fear overrode muscular issues and I increased pace, then jumped for the lowest branch on the tree.

Because of my speed when I grabbed the tree, my entire body swung up, and I pulled an Olympic gymnast move, swinging up, tucking in, and banging my waist over the branch. Okay, so maybe the banging part wasn't exactly Olympic quality, but since Olympians were rarely performing for their lives, I was giving it a pass.

Without even pausing, I pushed myself up from the branch and scrambled to the next one up, wanting to put at least ten feet of distance between me and the charging animal. When I was firmly planted on the limb, I looked down and saw the alligator standing at the bottom of the tree, hissing, my cell phone lying beside him. It must have fallen out when I pulled my gymnastic move into the tree.

I felt my waistband and groaned when I remembered I'd left my pistol in my Jeep. If anything was a sure sign I was done with the CIA, this was it. I used to wear that pistol like underwear. I did have a DoubleTap in my sock, but that was only two nine- millimeter rounds. I didn't know much about alligators, but I'd seen something on television that said you killed them by shooting a small spot on the back of their heads. Two bullets and my sketchy television recall didn't seem like much of an offense against the monster below, but what other options did I have?

I reached down for the pistol, then hesitated. The alligator had been in Gertie's bathtub, literally taking a soak. No way he'd walked in from the swamp, strolled through her front door, and run a bath. Which meant Gertie was up to something, and I had a sneaking suspicion that the alligator was the source of the emergency text. Of course, now it had morphed into a whole different emergency than the one Gertie had called about.

"What the hell are you doing up there?" Ida Belle's voice rang out from the porch. "And what happened to the screen door?"

I looked over at the perplexed Ida Belle and realized that the alligator was positioned behind a stack of mulch, making him not visible from Ida Belle's position on the porch.

"Move ten feet to your right and look under the tree," I yelled.

The alligator hissed again, and I gave him the finger.

Ida Belle shook her head and walked to the far end of the porch. When she caught sight of the alligator, her eyes widened. "Good Lord, what the hell has that woman gotten up to now?"

"She's gotten me up a tree, for starters. And she's going to need a new screen door and I'm not paying for it. Beyond that, I've got nothing."

"You've got a gun, don't you?"

"Of course."

"Then shoot the dang thing. Unless you want to hang out in a tree all day. I'm pretty sure he can wait you out."

"I thought about it, but I was afraid *this* was the

emergency."

"Looks like an emergency from where I'm standing."

"I mean the emergency Gertie called us over here for. This thing was in her bathtub. I opened the door thinking Gertie had fallen and needed help, and now we're here."

Ida Belle frowned. "Where is Gertie, anyway?"

A wave of panic rushed through me. "You don't think the gator ate her, do you?"

Ida Belle studied the alligator for a bit longer than I found comfortable, then shook her head. "He's too small. Besides, he'd want her dead for a couple days before he started chewing on her. They like their meat aged a bit."

"The only meat in Sinful older than Gertie is Sheriff Lee."

Ida Belle nodded appreciatively. "That's a good one, and I give you additional points for making the joke under stress. Plus, it's hard to get a funny one in about decomposition."

"This conversation is really grossing me out. Find Gertie or I'm shooting this thing and grilling it up for dinner."

Ida Belle walked back into the house and I could hear her calling for Gertie. I believed Ida Belle was correct when she said the gator was too small to eat someone, but that didn't mean he hadn't injured her enough to kill her, then left her to rot in one of the upstairs rooms. I'd seen a video on YouTube of an alligator climbing a hurricane fence. If they could manage fences, then stairs wouldn't be a problem. He certainly hadn't had a problem going down the porch steps.

I broke off a dead branch from the limb next to me and threw it at the alligator, hoping I could scare him into moving back. If I could get a decent head start, I could get away. The only caveat was that I had no idea where to go. The house was out of the question. That bathroom door hadn't even put a dent in the gator's stride. And it was a long sprint through the house to my Jeep. Not to mention having to open the front door. I could hardly go running through that one like I had the screen.

I was just about to decide that Ida Belle was never coming back when she stepped out onto the porch and shrugged. "She's not in there. Her purse is on the counter. Car is in the garage, but no sign of her."

"Did you try calling?"

"Of course I tried calling. Her phone is in her purse."

"Well, I've got a leg cramp and haven't had a cup of coffee. I'm shooting it."

Ida Belle waved one hand at the gator. "No arguments here."

I pulled the pistol out of my sock and leaned over the branch to get a direct shot at the spot I needed to pierce. I was just about to squeeze the trigger when Gertie bolted out the back door yelling.

"Don't shoot!"

Chapter Seven

As she ran for the steps, she tripped on the remnants of the screen and tumbled down the porch stairs, rolling herself up in the screen as she went. By the time she came to a stop in the lawn, she looked like a spring roll or a burrito, depending on your food preferences.

The alligator whirled around and took off at a fast walk in her direction. Ida Belle yelled at me to shoot, but I didn't have a good angle to pull off a shot; I leaned out from the tree and took one shot, but as I pulled the trigger, the limb I was leaning against snapped and I fired high, shooting a hole through Gertie's kitchen window.

I struggled for a second, trying to keep my balance, but gravity won and I pitched out of the tree and hit the ground. I managed to roll as I hit, bounced up, and took off after the alligator.

"I don't have a clear shot," I yelled as I ran.

Ida Belle had scrambled down the stairs and was trying to untangle Gertie from her wire cocoon. Gertie had been yelling the entire time, but everything was garbled, probably because a mess of wire was pulling her face in four different directions.

As the alligator inched closer, Ida Belle yelled at me again to shoot, but he was too far ahead for me to get a good angle. I couldn't kill it, but maybe I could distract it. I said a quick prayer and fired the last shot at its tail. The alligator stopped running and threw its head around. I swear it was glaring at me.

"Run the other way," Ida Belle yelled.

I waited until the beast started my direction, then took off running across the yard for the back fence. Then I saw the door open on Gertie's toolshed. I glanced back and saw the alligator gaining on me. I shifted right and increased pace toward the shed. I was about twenty feet ahead of the gator when I bolted inside and shoved up the window on the back. The gator ran in the shed behind me, taking out an entire row of flowerpots on a bottom shelf as he lunged for me.

I vaulted onto the workbench and launched out the window and onto the roof. I scurried to the other side, flipped off, and slammed the shed door shut, then slid the bolt in place, locking the angry alligator inside. I took a second to admire my handiwork, then set off for the house, where Ida Belle was still struggling to get Gertie free from the screen.

"I need wire cutters," Ida Belle said. "This crap is all entwined."

The screen was wrapped around Gertie from her head all the way down to her butt, leaving only her legs dangling out. She was still trying to talk, but with the way the screen had her face contorted, everything was garbled.

"Let me guess," I said. "The wire cutters are in the shed."

"Of course, but this is thin enough that I can make do with kitchen shears. Just help me get her inside in case that thing comes bursting out of there."

As if on cue, we heard a loud bang. We both whirled around and watched as the door on the shed shook.

"That door is made of plywood," I said. "It's not going to hold him long."

"Upsy-daisy," Ida Belle said.

We grabbed Gertie's screen-covered shoulders and pulled

her to a standing position. Another bang rang out, and this time a splintering sound followed. I looked back and saw the alligator's head emerge from the bottom of the splintered door.

"Time's up!" I yelled.

We grabbed Gertie's shoulders and half pulled her up the steps and dashed across the porch. Her legs were moving as fast as they could go, but her balance was worse than ever due to being wrapped up like a burrito. We got her to the door but as she ran inside, she tripped over the threshold and crashed onto the floor. I looked back and saw the gator only thirty feet away and closing the distance rapidly.

I bolted inside behind Ida Belle and tried to slam the door, but couldn't because the lump that was Gertie was blocking the opening. I reached down to try to pull her out of the way, certain I'd never get her moved in time, when Ida Belle placed her foot right on Gertie's hip and shoved as hard as she could.

Gertie rolled out of the doorway and I slammed the door just in time to stop the charging animal from entering the house. Gertie kept going into the breakfast nook and took out a floor lamp. The alligator slammed against the door once, but this one was hurricane-proof and wasn't going to go as easily as the others. He tried one more time, then slunk off the porch and stared at the back door.

Ida Belle grabbed a pair of kitchen shears and started cutting the screen away from Gertie, beginning at the bottom.

"Why aren't you starting with her head?" I asked.

"Because I'm certain this crazy woman brought that alligator here, and I want to tell her just how stupid it was without her interrupting."

It sounded reasonable to me, so I flopped into a chair where I had a view of the backyard, and our friend the gator, and held the loose piece of screen as Ida Belle cut, unraveled, and ranted.

"You've officially lost your mind," Ida Belle said. "I've thought it before, and always gave you the benefit of the doubt, but this time, I'm certain. As soon as I get you out of this wrapper, I'm driving you to New Orleans to be fitted for a permanent one in white. You are a danger to society and more importantly, to Fortune and me. What the hell were you thinking?"

Ida Belle clipped through the last of the screen as she finished her diatribe. Gertie sat up and moved her lips around, probably trying to get some blood circulating back in them. Her face was a mess of red grid lines. It looked like someone had beaten her with a flyswatter.

"Are you okay?" I asked, figuring someone probably should and Ida Belle didn't appear to be in any mood for it.

"I'm fine," Gertie said, and glared at Ida Belle. "And I'm not crazy. I have a perfectly good reason for having Godzilla here."

Ida Belle shook her head. "Good God, she's named it."

"Unless the reason for having that alligator includes a barbecue," I said, "I am going to go ahead and call BS on the perfectly good reason thing."

Gertie rose from the floor and headed into the kitchen. "I've got to have something to drink. My mouth tastes like rust."

"If you'd changed that screen when I told you to," Ida Belle said, "it wouldn't taste bad."

"Well, since I wasn't planning on eating it," Gertie said, "I wasn't concerned about the taste."

She pulled a soda out of the refrigerator, plopped down on a barstool, and took a big drink. I glanced over at Ida Belle, who wore her impatience on her face as clearly as she did her nose. I was getting a little miffed myself. No one liked to sprint for their life first thing in the morning. Especially without coffee.

"Out with it," Ida Belle said. "Fortune hasn't had coffee and that's never a good thing."

Gertie's eyes widened and she jumped off the stool. "No coffee? I'll put some on."

Ida Belle pointed her finger at Gertie. "If you take one step toward that coffeepot, I will kill you with the remnants of that floor lamp. What the hell are you doing with that alligator?"

"Saving him," Gertie said.

"For a barbecue?" I asked.

"No! I'm saving him from the poacher."

Suddenly, the pieces fell together and everything made sense…in a Gertie sort of way. The solitary fishing trips, the giant bait, leaning over the boat gazing into the water, whatever horrible thing was cooking in the oven.

"So let me get this straight," I said. "You brought that thing here to make sure the poacher didn't get it, and putting it in your bathtub seemed like a good idea. Not that any of this was a good idea, but inside your house? Front door open? Emergency text for me and Ida Belle to show up? What did you think would happen?"

Ida Belle nodded. "And where were you, anyway? This might not have gotten out of control if you'd been here telling people not to open the bathroom door."

"So many questions," Gertie said. "I'm already confused."

"Skip everything Fortune asked," Ida Belle said. "Since it all questions your decision-making ability when it comes to logic, the questions are moot. Where were you?"

"I was at Melba's house. They went fishing last night and I asked her to save me the scraps after they filleted the fish. She had a bag for me but wanted it out of her backyard because it was starting to stink the place up."

Ida Belle wrinkled her nose. "Like whatever is in the oven is stinking your kitchen up? Don't tell me you're baking fish parts?"

Gertie crossed her arms. "I'm making a fish casserole, if you must know."

Ida Belle stared. "You're baking a casserole for an alligator? I have officially heard it all. He eats fish and dead things. What makes you think he'd want a casserole?"

"The first time he swam up to my boat, I gave him half of my ham sandwich. Then another time I gave him leftover pizza and sugar cookies. He really seemed to like the baked stuff, so I figured a casserole of fish made sense."

"I'm sure in your world, it does." Ida Belle sighed. "Should I even ask how you got that thing to your house?"

"I rigged up a pulley to the light bar on my boat and hoisted him up," Gertie said. "Then I backed the Caddy down the boat ramp and plopped him in the trunk. I broke the rest of the bottom out of the trunk when I got into the garage and he fell right out."

"How did you get the hook out of his mouth?" I asked.

Gertie looked horrified. "I didn't hook him. I made a sling out of a couple pairs of old pants."

I looked over at Ida Belle, but she appeared as confused as I was. "And the alligator let you strap him with pants? Like it was completely normal?"

"I suppose it's not normal," Gertie said, "but that's what I was trying to tell you when I was wrapped up in the screen— Godzilla won't hurt me. He was probably coming to protect me."

Ida Belle pulled her cell phone from her pocket. "That does it. I'm calling the state mental hospital."

Gertie grabbed a handful of cookies off a plate on the kitchen counter and headed for the door. "See for yourself."

I started to stop her, but Ida Belle waved one hand at me and pulled a .45 out of Gertie's purse with the other. We followed Gertie onto the porch, and the alligator looked up at us and flicked his tail back and forth. And sure enough, he was staring right at Gertie. She started down the steps and I began to panic.

"That's far enough," I said when she was halfway down.

The gator was only five feet away. Ida Belle was a crack shot, but any closer and safety would have been questionable given how quickly the alligator could move. Gertie tossed a cookie at the gator and he opened his mouth and caught it midair, then chomped on it a time or two before opening his mouth again, apparently wanting seconds. Gertie obliged with another cookie until she was down to the last one. Then she jumped off the remaining two steps and leaned over to drop the last cookie in the gator's mouth before climbing back up the stairs to stand between Ida Belle and me.

"Holy crap," I said. "Surely there's a law about feeding alligators cookies or having alligators in your home or something."

Despite the gator's seemingly passive view of Gertie, I didn't trust it for a second. Sinful had all sorts of odd laws, and if one of them got the gator off her property and back in the bayou where it belonged, then I was all for it.

"There's all sorts of laws about this sort of thing," Ida Belle said. "Mostly state. You can't just take protected wildlife home for a visit and you darned sure can't keep him."

"It's just until the poacher's caught," Gertie argued.

"But does he have to stay here?" I asked. "Can't you put the pants back on him and relocate him away from Sinful?"

Gertie shook her head. "Alligators are territorial. I can't just drop him somewhere else. It would be like dropping a Crip off in

Blood territory."

Somehow, I didn't think alligators fell into the same pattern as LA gangs, but I sorta got the point. "What about a wildlife refuge? Even you have to agree that you can't keep him in your house."

"Of course not," Gertie said. "That's what I needed you guys for. I have an old plastic pond liner that I was going to use to make him a place to get in water in the yard. I just need a hole big enough to put it in."

"You called us over here, on emergency status, to dig a hole for an alligator pond?" Ida Belle asked. "Just put the liner on the ground, throw in some water, and pitch his butt over in it."

"The edge is about a foot and a half high," Gertie said. "He might hurt himself getting in and out."

"He just ran through a bathroom door and a shed," I said. "I think he can manage a one-foot drop onto grass or into water."

"He ran through the bathroom door?" Gertie asked.

I stared. "Yeah. Do you think I opened the door and invited him to play tag?"

Ida Belle shook her head. "When Carter finds out you've got a gator in your backyard, you know he's going to haul it right back into the bayou."

"He won't find out if we don't tell him," Gertie said.

I held up my hands. "Oh, rest assured, I'm not about to offer up this debacle, but your neighbors can see into your backyard. And I'm going to go ahead and guess that they won't look favorably on your new choice of pets, especially when I've been shooting at it."

"Given that they've known Gertie for decades," Ida Belle said, "they'll probably call when she starts digging the hole, even if they didn't see any of the rest."

JANA DELEON

Gertie put her hands on her hips. "You have one little miscalculation with explosives and everyone's a critic. How was I supposed to know the hole needed to be twice as deep?"

Since most of Gertie's yard looked professionally landscaped, I'd always wondered about the somewhat bare spot off to the right. I guess I'd gotten my answer. I looked at Ida Belle, who was staring at the gator and frowning, and then at Gertie, who was staring at the gator and I swear was starting to tear up.

Damn it. I knew I was going to regret it, but before I could change my mind, I blurted out, "Why don't you keep him at my house? The bayou is right there. If he's really as tame as you think, he won't go far, right? If he does, then so be it. You can't change nature and you shouldn't try to."

Gertie perked up. "Will you feed him?"

"Heck no, I won't feed him. I may never go in the backyard again. And I'll have to reinforce my doors."

"I can come over and feed him every day." Gertie's eyes widened. "Oh, even better, I could stay with you until this has all blown over. That way, I'd be on hand to make sure Godzilla doesn't misbehave."

"Who's going to make sure you don't misbehave?" Ida Belle asked.

"I'm not a child," Gertie said, "and besides, it's Fortune's house. She's in charge."

"I don't know," I said. "My only experience in dealing with those who misbehave has been to shoot them. I really don't want to shoot you."

"You two drive me crazy." Gertie spun around and headed into the house. "I'm going to take that casserole out and feed Godzilla. He'll travel better with a full stomach."

Ida Belle looked at me and sighed. "What in the world have

you gotten yourself into now?"

"Trouble. But that's nothing new."

───

It was one thing to offer my backyard to house Gertie's alligator. It was a whole other issue figuring out how to get the gator to my yard. The trunk of Gertie's car was completely gone now, so that option was out. Ida Belle would have allowed Celia to drive her new vehicle before she let an alligator in it, and my Jeep was completely open, so no way of hiding what we were doing.

And hiding was the most important part of this mission. Hiding and not dying.

A search of Gertie's yard and a little ingenuity produced a plan. Not a great plan, but it was better than carrying the thing down the middle of the street wrapped in a sheet. That might attract attention.

In the back of Gertie's shed was an odd sort of boat canoe thingie. Ida Belle called it a peerow, but I figured I must have heard wrong. That didn't sound like a good name for a boat at all. Regardless, it was long enough to hold the alligator and had sides high enough to camouflage Godzilla as long as he stayed put. It sat on a small trailer that could be easily pulled behind my Jeep so all that was left was to get the gator in the peerow, cover it up, take it to my house, and get it in the backyard before anyone noticed what we were doing.

Simple.

Unless, of course, you're trying to shove a live alligator into a boat and get it through a suburb without being seen.

Gertie distracted Godzilla with a loaf of bread, and we hauled the peerow out of the shed and into the backyard. Once it was in place, and we were a safe distance away from Godzilla, I had to ask. "Okay, I get the 'row' part of the name, but what's with the 'pee'? I refuse to accept that you mean that literally."

Ida Belle looked at Gertie, and they started to laugh.

"It's spelled p-i-r-o-g-u-e," Ida Belle said. "It's one of those words the Cajuns adopted, hence the pronunciation. Think of it as Cajun for canoe."

I had zero idea how one got "peerow" from "pirogue," but I wasn't about to get into a language discussion, especially over anything that people in Louisiana had adjusted to suit themselves. With all the cultures mixed together, that path would produce nothing but more confusion.

I looked at the gator and the pirogue. "How are we going to get him in it? I don't think he's going to voluntarily climb in, even for a cookie."

"We can lift him in," Gertie said. "He's not that heavy."

"I'm not putting my hands on that thing," Ida Belle said. "Fortune's cat ran across my foot last week and it bled for a good fifteen minutes. That thing's claws would shred a foot clean off."

"We'll use the pants sling, like I did before," Gertie said. "There's a couple tears in it from the trip here, but nothing I can't patch with a little thread."

"You want to take time out to sew?" Ida Belle asked. "Grab some duct tape and let's get this over with."

Ten minutes and a roll of duct tape later, we had a sorta sturdy sling that might possibly, I hoped, hold the alligator. Now all we had to do was get the pants under the gator, which I was guessing had been a whole lot easier when he was floating on water.

"I can't be the only one wondering how we're going to get the pants under the gator, right?" I asked.

"I've been thinking about that," Gertie said. "I think the

easiest way would be if you lift his tail until his back legs are off the ground, then I'll shove the pants under and Ida Belle can pull them through to the other side."

The entire mess sounded more and more ridiculous the longer we plodded along, but five minutes later, the gator was munching on fish casserole, and I was straining to get half of him high enough for the pants squad to get the sling in place. It probably only took them a couple seconds, but it felt like I'd been holding him up forever before I finally plopped him back down on the lawn. Godzilla was so busy with the nasty casserole he hadn't even looked back to see why his hind end was dangling in midair.

I rubbed my shoulders and arms and shook my head. "Guys, I don't think we can lift him into the pirogue. It was all I could do to get the tail up. There's a lot more gator to lift."

Ida Belle studied the gator and the pirogue. "Maybe we could turn the pirogue on its side and drag the gator in partway, then flip it over."

"And if he decided he doesn't like flipping and he comes jumping out and chasing people up trees again?" I asked.

"Then we go inside and call Carter and he sends the people who will put him back into the bayou where he belongs," Ida Belle said. "Sans pants, of course." She looked over at Gertie. "And no arguments from you."

"Fine," Gertie said. "If we can't make it work, then I'll turn him over to Carter."

I didn't think for a moment Gertie would let go of it that easily, but since the gator was wrapped up in a sling, I figured that gave me enough of a head start to get out if things went south and Ida Belle started shooting. I hadn't missed the fact that she'd stuck Gertie's .45 in her pocket.

I directed Ida Belle to grab the other end of the pirogue and we turned it on its side and moved it next to the alligator. Then Ida Belle got on the back side of the pirogue, and I handed her one end of the pants to pull and lift with. Gertie and I got on the other side and each grabbed a wad of polyester.

I started the countdown. "On three. One. Two. Three!"

The gator weighed a bit less that I'd expected. Apparently, they carry a lot of weight in their tail, so when we heaved, he moved more than anticipated. We lifted him clean off the ground and into the side of the pirogue so hard and fast that he banged into the bottom and flipped the whole thing over. Ida Belle managed to leap out of the way just as the pirogue came crashing down on the ground, and she hopped back up, hand at her waist as we all stared at the alligator.

He tossed his head from side to side, banging it on the pirogue, then wiggled around until he was positioned comfortably down the center, then closed his eyes.

"He's going to sleep," I said. "I don't believe it. It's almost like he knows we're trying to help him."

"Don't you get carried away on that crap," Ida Belle said. "The last thing I need is two of you ascribing human emotions to a prehistoric reptile. More likely, his digestive system is wondering what the heck he's done to it and has put him down for the count until it figures something out."

"Either way," I said, "let's get this covered with the tarp, slide it up on the trailer, and get out of here before one of the neighbors calls Carter and tattles."

"Too late." Carter's voice sounded on the porch behind us.

Chapter Eight

I whirled around, trying to come up with a cover story, but my inventory of smuggling-alligators-in-pirogues tales was completely empty. Gertie and Ida Belle didn't appear to be doing any better. They both stared at Carter, their brows scrunched in concentration.

"No one?" he asked. "Unbelievable. The first time I've seen all three of you speechless."

"That's because none of us can come up with a decent lie," I said.

"That statement should bother me," he said, "but coming from you, it makes perfect sense. I'm not even going to ask you what you're doing, because no way in hell do I want to know. What I'm going to do is tell you to get that gator back into the bayou before someone calls Wildlife and Fisheries and they arrest you for poaching."

Crap. I hadn't even thought about that angle of this mess.

"I guess now isn't a good time to be caught with an alligator in your backyard," I said. "I mean, if you live on the bayou then maybe, but since it's wrapped up in pants and sitting in a pirogue, that would probably look suspicious."

Carter raised one eyebrow. "You think? Look, I already have the state stepping all over my toes on this one. The last thing I need is the three of you arrested over whatever this is."

"I was just—" Gertie started to explain, but Carter held a

hand up to cut her off.

"I said I didn't want to know." He pointed at the pirogue. "In the water, now."

"That's exactly where we were going," Ida Belle said.

Carter looked at the three of us, clearly not convinced.

"I swear on Francine's banana pudding," Ida Belle said.

That seemed to mollify him. "Fine," he said. "Then hurry."

"It would go faster if you'd help us slide the pirogue on the trailer," I said.

He sighed. "Great. Then I can be party to the illegal act. That's exactly what I need."

We all ignored his completely accurate statement and pulled the tarp over the pirogue, securing it on the sides with duct tape. I positioned the trailer in front of the pirogue, and Carter and I grabbed the front of the boat with Ida Belle and Gertie pushing from the end. I tipped the trailer back and we tugged until the pirogue was in place, then I drove my Jeep through the wide gate on the side yard and we hooked the trailer up.

"This trailer is rusted pretty bad," Carter said. "I don't know how long it's going to hold up, so don't drive fast."

"We're just taking Godzilla to—" Gertie started, and Carter held up his hand again.

"Don't want to know where you're going," he said. "Don't want to know why you've named an alligator. Don't want to know why he's wrapped in pants. I already have to forget all of this on the way to my truck and come up with something to tell your neighbors."

He whirled around and stalked out of the backyard. Gertie, Ida Belle, and I headed for the Jeep, Ida Belle riding shotgun, or .45 as the case was, and Gertie sitting in the back, watching the trailer. I pulled out of the backyard and onto the street, cringing when the trailer banged as the tires rolled off the curb.

"It's still holding up," Gertie said, "and Godzilla hasn't moved."

I let out a breath of relief. "We can do this, right? It's only a few blocks."

"Famous last words," Ida Belle said.

And we almost made it.

A block from my house, I stopped at the corner and was preparing to turn when two teens roared out of a driveway in an enormous truck with ridiculous wheels and barreled down the road in front of us, blaring a horn that sounded like an ocean liner. We all froze, then whirled around to look at the trailer. At first, it appeared we'd escaped unscathed, then we heard a loud thump, and the pirogue shook. The second thump was even harder and this time, the top of the tarp flew up, pulling a section of duct tape loose.

I whirled around and floored it, squealing around the corner and racing for my house. I glanced at the rearview mirror and saw the pirogue jumping back and forth on the trailer, and I prayed that the rusted piece of metal would hold long enough to get us to my backyard. I hit my driveway at an angle, attempting to get the trailer up the slope rather than jumping the curb, but I was only partially successful.

I looked in the rearview and saw the alligator's head shoot out of the pirogue, tearing the tarp loose on the front of the boat. The wind caught the tarp and ripped it completely off. I steered across the driveway and into the yard, headed for the side of the house. If I could make it around back, then it would just be a matter of getting the gator into the water.

"The hitch is breaking," Gertie yelled. "If you make another turn, it will break off."

"Hold on!" I yelled as I drove into the backyard and straight at the bayou. Ida Belle secured her seat belt and Gertie flopped around, grabbing the roll bar. I floored the Jeep and just a couple feet before I reached the water, I made a hard right turn.

I heard the trailer hitch snap as it broke away from the Jeep. Free of the additional weight, the Jeep leaped ahead tossing us all back against our seats before I slammed on the brakes, flinging us forward. We all turned around and watched as the broken trailer ran straight into the bayou. The alligator, seeing that home was in sight, clawed his way over the side of the pirogue and disappeared in the murky water.

The front half of the pirogue had come loose when it hit the water and was trying to float off with the current. The back end was still attached to the submerged trailer.

"We have to get that out of the water before someone sees it," I said.

Ida Belle nodded. "Someone being Carter."

"We can put a rope around it and haul it backward into the lawn," Gertie said. "Even without the hitch, we should be able to wrangle some way to get it back to my house. It's not that heavy without the gator."

"The problem is not getting it back to your house," I said. "I could walk it back to your house. The problem is getting a rope on it because I am not getting in the water with that thing. I barely have an advantage on land. I'm not wandering into his house after we hacked him off."

"That gator is probably long gone," Ida Belle said.

"Really?" I asked. "Then you won't mind securing the rope."

"No way," Ida Belle said. "This is Gertie's mess. She can secure the rope. I'll stand ready to shoot."

Now that the gator was back in the water, Gertie didn't look as sure of her scaly friend as she had before. "Fine," she said finally, and grabbed a rope I kept behind the backseat of the

Jeep. She climbed over the side and headed for the bayou. Ida Belle jumped out and stood at the shoreline, pistol drawn. I backed the Jeep up to the bank.

"Tie it off to the Jeep first," I said. I didn't add the part about, in case something happened, we still had the rope.

Gertie looped the rope around the hitch and then walked to the edge of the bayou. She scanned the surface, looking for any sign of the alligator, but the only movement on the water was the outgoing tide. She clutched the other end of the rope, a determined look on her face, and marched into the water.

"Tie it off anywhere on the trailer," I said. "Just get a good knot and get the heck out of there. I'll drag it up the bank."

Gertie nodded as she bent over and stuck the rope under the water. A boat passed by on the bayou, not bothering to slow, and Ida Belle yelled at them.

"Watch for the wake," Ida Belle said as the waves created by the passing boat rolled in.

"I'm almost done," Gertie said. "Got it!"

She rose up to leave just as the first wave hit her. It wasn't that big so I didn't anticipate any issues, but all of a sudden, Gertie's eyes widened and she screamed.

"It's got me! Lord, help me! It's got me!"

I jumped out of the Jeep yelling at Ida Belle to shoot.

"I can't see anything," Ida Belle said, waving the gun at the surface of the water surrounding Gertie.

Gertie attempted to bolt forward, but one leg didn't go along with the rest of her body and she pitched face-first into the bayou. Ida Belle tossed the gun on the bank, and we both dashed into the water to help Gertie up and pulled her onto the bank.

"I'm going to bleed out and die," Gertie cried. "Did I loose the leg?"

Ida Belle grabbed the gun and scanned the shore, and I

checked Gertie for injuries. Then I saw the polyester pants wrapped around her ankle and trailing into the water, where I would bet money they had been caught on the trailer.

"Your leg is fine," I said as I leaned over and pulled the pants off her ankle. "You're tangled in the pants. The alligator didn't bite you. If he heard you scream, he's probably halfway to Florida."

Ida Belle shoved the gun in her waistband and walked back up the bank, shaking her head. "You have got to work on that panicking thing. So much drama."

Gertie flipped over and eyed her legs, as if she didn't quite believe me. Once she was convinced that there was no bite, no blood loss, and probably wouldn't even be a bruise, she rose from the ground.

"Pull this thing out of the water," she said. "What are you standing around for? I might want to use that pirogue sometime."

Before I could even open my mouth to reply, Ida Belle pulled out the pistol and fired a hole in the front of the pirogue.

Gertie shot her a look of dismay. "What did you do that for?"

Ida Belle shoved the gun back in her jeans. "Because I had the overwhelming urge to shoot something, and I couldn't shoot you. Besides, the last thing you need to do with that awful balance of yours is get on the water in a pirogue. You'd think every piece of marsh grass in the bayou was trying to drown you."

Ida Belle stepped to the side and waved a hand at me. "Drag that heap out of the water. It's already midday and if I don't get food soon, I'm going to get grouchy."

Since the apparently not-yet-grouchy Ida Belle had just shot a hole in an innocent pirogue, I figured it was best to get moving while she was still in a good mood. I jumped in the Jeep and dragged the trailer out of the water, then went to inspect the situation.

"This is no big deal," I said. "I can put a strap around the trailer tongue and wrap it around the hitch. I won't have any problem getting it to your house."

Gertie nodded but didn't turn around to look at trailer. She was standing at the edge of the bayou, scanning the surface. "Do you think Godzilla is all right?"

"That alligator is doing a lot better than the three of us," Ida Belle said.

"I hope I fed him enough," Gertie said. "I wouldn't want him to get hungry."

"Unless he can tote a .45," Ida Belle said, "you should worry more about *my* hunger."

Gertie stepped away from the bank and waved a hand. "All this complaining. As soon as we get to my house, I'll whip up a casserole."

"No!" Ida Belle and I sounded off together.

Thirty minutes later, Ida Belle and I flopped into chairs at Francine's Café. I felt like I'd run a marathon and sat through one of Pastor Don's sermons. The exhaustion was real. Ida Belle didn't look any better than I did. Gertie had refused to come, insisting that she needed to pack up some things and get back to my house as soon as possible in case Godzilla showed up. She wanted to make sure he knew where to hang out.

Great. If that gator returned, I was officially done using my backyard.

Neither Ida Belle nor I had the energy to change clothes, and we were both still dripping a little from our jaunt into the bayou to rescue Gertie from the grasp of the terrible, awful polyester pants monster. Ally walked up to the table and gave us a critical eye.

"You two look like you've put in a week just this morning," she said.

"You have no idea," I said.

"Gertie?" Ally asked.

"How did you guess?" I asked.

"Well, she's not here, for one thing," Ally said, "and Ida Belle's wearing that sorta constipated look she gets when she's feeling exasperated about something Gertie's done that she doesn't agree with."

"I must look constipated a lot," Ida Belle said.

Ally grinned. "I would love to offer you a drink, but town laws and all. How about a root beer? It has a little bite to it."

Ida Belle pulled a bottle of cough syrup from her pocket. "Just bring Coke. I've got the rest covered."

"And a lots of bread and butter," I said.

Ally nodded and hurried off, returning a minute later with a big basket of bread and two huge servings of butter, then took our lunch order. Ida Belle and I requested two entrées each and then dived into the bread like we'd just spent ten days in the desert.

I took a huge bite and processed it, then sighed. "This might be the longest I've gone without food since I've been here."

Ida Belle nodded. "Until the big fish debacle of 1963, it was illegal to skip a meal."

For a split second, I thought about asking what exactly a fish debacle entailed, but I really liked eating fish and was sort of afraid of the answer. "What if you were sick?"

"Special dispensation, but you needed a doctor's note."

I shook my head and shoved another piece of bread in my mouth. Sinful had the most ridiculous laws I'd ever heard. I couldn't imagine any of them were constitutional, but approximately two months of experience with the town had taught me that clearly, Sinful was okay with the absurd. In fact, the town almost seemed to encourage it as some badge of honor.

I was working on my third piece of bread when I heard shouting outside. We were seated in front of the plate glass window, so I had a clear view of the ruckus. A man stood in the doorway of the sheriff's department, his hand balled in a fist and waving in the air. His face was red, and his whole body shook with anger. Carter stood in front of him, clearly frustrated, but all he did was nod as the man ranted.

"That's Quincy Hebert," Ida Belle said. "He's one of Gertie's third or fourth cousins."

"Is he always that angry?"

"I've known Quincy his entire life and have never heard him raise his voice. Not even when he should have. We better go see what's wrong."

We headed outside and across the street. As we approached the sidewalk in front of the sheriff's department, Quincy slammed the door in Carter's face, whirled around, and stalked off the sidewalk and into the street.

Six feet four. Two hundred forty pounds of mostly muscle. Was probably good in a fistfight, but I could outrun him.

"Quincy?" Ida Belle called out.

He gave a start, and I realized that he was so angry he hadn't even seen us standing there when he'd walked by.

"Ida Belle," he said, and his face softened a bit as he focused on her. "I'm sorry. I'm so mad I can't see straight."

"What's wrong?" Ida Belle asked.

"You've heard about the alligator poaching?" he asked.

97

We both nodded.

"Well, that idiot game warden arrested Petey, and Carter won't let him loose."

"What?!"

Ida Belle's expression and tone was filled with so much incredulity that whoever Petey was, I gathered he wasn't capable of the poaching.

Quincy flung his arms in the air. "What the heck am I supposed to do? That boy can't stay in a cell."

"Carter knows better," Ida Belle said. "Why won't he turn Petey loose?"

"He said he's been on the phone with the state for an hour now and they refuse to give him permission to let Petey go, even though he'd be releasing him into my custody. Says his job is on the line."

Ida Belle frowned. "And the state trumps everything. What kind of evidence do they have?"

"Carter said they wouldn't tell him, but the state insisted that it's enough to hold Petey and that Carter had better do as he was told." Quincy gave Ida Belle a pained look. "I don't want Carter to lose his job, but I can't let my boy stay there alone."

I still didn't understand exactly what was going on. The expression "my boy" could mean that Petey was Quincy's son or it could mean he was a good friend. And I had no idea why Petey couldn't manage sitting alone in a jail cell, but maybe he was claustrophobic. The jail part of the building was rather small and had poor lighting.

"Maybe you can stay there with him," Ida Belle said.

"I already asked," Quincy said. "Carter said the cells are full—some party got out of hand at the Swamp Bar last night and Deputy Breaux filled the place up with drunk idiots."

"Petey's not locked up with those barbarians?" Ida Belle

looked horrified.

Quincy shook his head. "Carter's got him in the storeroom for now, but even when he gets the drunks cleared out, he says he can't let a civilian stay inside. Celia's already been around and let him know she's watching. Any sign of rule-breaking and he's out."

"This election recount needs to finish and in Marie's favor." I looked at Quincy. "So basically, you can't go to jail unless you break the law."

"That's what it looks like," Quincy said.

"Hit me," I said.

Quincy stared at me as if I'd lost my mind. "What?"

"Hit me," I repeated. "It doesn't have to be hard. Hell, grab my arm. Whatever."

Ida Belle's eyes widened, and she nodded. "Do it, Quincy."

"You two have lost your minds," Quincy said.

"You need a legitimate reason to be in jail," I said. "I'm going to give you one, and then when push comes to shove, I'll refuse to press charges."

Quincy's face cleared in understanding, and he looked back and forth between Ida Belle and me. "You're sure?"

"Yep," I said, "but on further thought, do the grabbing thing. You look like you pack a mean punch."

He reached out and grabbed my arm and I was really happy I'd opted out of the punch. He had a grip like a vise, and I was fairly certain I'd have some bruises to show for it.

"Help! Stop!" I screamed. "Now let go," I whispered.

Quincy let go of me and dropped his arms to his sides. A couple seconds later, Carter rushed out of the sheriff's department and stared at the three of us. "Did one of you yell?" he asked.

"I did," I said, clutching my arm. "This man assaulted me."

Carter's jaw dropped. "What?"

"You heard her," Ida Belle said. "We were trying to talk some sense into Quincy, and he grabbed Fortune's arm like he was going to wrestle her to the ground."

I turned to the side and removed my hand. "See," I said, pointing to the red marks on my biceps.

Carter stared at Quincy in dismay. "What the hell are you thinking?"

"I don't care what he's thinking," Ida Belle said. "What I think is that you need to arrest this man and lock him up until he calms down. He's a danger to society."

Carter's eye narrowed at me. "Is that what you want? For me to arrest Quincy?"

"I think it would be wise," I said. "It would have been a lot worse if he'd grabbed someone less fit than me. He could have broken their arm."

"Uh-huh," Carter said. "And you'll come in and file a complaint?"

"Ida Belle and I haven't eaten all day," I said. "Can it wait until after lunch? Our food should be up now."

"Okay," Carter said. "I don't need you passing out on me. Finish up your lunch and have a doctor take a look at that arm. I don't want to be accused of holding injured people in the sheriff's department over paperwork. If you feel up to it after you've seen the doctor, then you can come back and file a report. Otherwise, I'll get it from you tomorrow or the day after. Quincy can stay put until then."

Carter waved a hand at Quincy, who turned and mouthed a "thank you" at me before lumbering into the sheriff's department. I could see the smile quivering on Carter's lips as he closed the door.

"That's way too many good deeds today before having a

decent meal," I said. "Let's go have lunch and you can tell me who Petey is and why I just encouraged a man to be arrested for assault."

"Let's get back into the café and get the gossiping over with," Ida Belle said, "then I'll fill you in."

We headed back into the café, where, as Ida Belle predicted, we were besieged by patrons wanting to know what happened. Ida Belle told them all that Quincy had some issue he was unhappy over and Carter was attempting to fix it, but neither had told us what the problem was. As Ida Belle had been blocking my body from café view when Quincy grabbed me, no one had seen the alleged assault.

The patrons gave Ida Belle a disappointed look, then went back to their conversations and meals. Ally came over with a huge tray of our lunch and started putting plates of hot food on the table.

"This sat on the hot plate for a bit," she said, "but I figured better a little dry than cold."

My mouth was already watering at the sight of the chicken-fried steak in front of me. It could have been as dry as cardboard and I wouldn't have cared. I grabbed the ketchup and poured it over the top, that whole gravy thing never catching on with me.

"I'll moisten it up," I said. "No worries here."

"None with me either," Ida Belle said. "I'm so hungry, I'd eat boiled tires if it had a decent sauce on top of it."

Ally laughed and set the last of the plates on the table. It was a four-top, and there was barely a square inch that wasn't covered. "The two of you are going to need a ride home on a flatbed trailer if you eat all of that," Ally said.

"I plan on eating all of it," I said, "and then ordering dessert."

Ida Belle nodded. "Plenty of folks with flatbed trailers

around here."

Ally nodded her head toward the window. "What was that about?"

Ida Belle looked around to make sure no one was within listening distance and leaned toward Ally, explaining what had happened. Ally's expression shifted from shocked, to outraged, to concerned.

"Poor Petey," Ally said. "I'm glad Quincy will be in with him. If there's anything I can do…"

"Maybe some lunch for Quincy, Petey, and Carter," Ida Belle said. "Put it on my tab."

"That's a great idea," Ally said. "The special today is pot roast and that's one of Petey's favorites. I'll make up some to-go orders right now and carry them over."

Ally hurried off to the kitchen, and I swallowed a bite of chicken-fried steak and looked over at Ida Belle. "Not to delay your eating process," I said, "but in between bites, can you please fill me in?"

Ida Belle nodded and downed a huge gulp of soda. "Petey is Quincy's son. He's nineteen but he's not quite right, so he's a very immature and sensitive nineteen."

"Autism?"

"No. I mean, not the traditional kind I don't think, although you'd need a doctor to explain it. He was in a horrible accident about six years ago and he's never been right since. He avoids people and rarely speaks when he comes across them, and he gets really upset at change."

"And I assume he wasn't like that before?"

"Not at all. Petey was one of the nicest, most outgoing kids you'd ever met. He was in every sport offered, made good grades, and spent every other waking moment fishing."

"What happened to him?"

"He and his best friend Reece Barron were in the bayou, cast-netting for bait fish. Reece threw the net over a submerged log and it got hung on the bottom. They couldn't get it undone from the boat, so Reece jumped in to get it loose from the log."

My heart thumped a bit harder as I braced myself for what was coming. "He drowned?"

"That was the official cause of death, but the drowning was caused by an alligator."

I sucked in a breath. "But you and Gertie said they mostly avoid people."

"They do, but this was a female with a nest nearby. Reece didn't stand a chance, really. She grabbed and rolled. By the time she let go and Petey got Reece back into the boat, he was already dead and Petey had been underwater for longer than a person should be."

"Oh my God. That poor kid."

I'd seen some horrible things as an adult, but I couldn't imagine, at thirteen, seeing your best friend mauled by an alligator and knowing there wasn't a thing you could do.

Ida Belle continued, "Petey tried CPR—most kids around here learn it fairly young—but he couldn't get a heartbeat. He heard a boat nearby and fired off a flare. It was Sheriff Lee, out fishing on his day off. He tried to resuscitate the boy as well, but couldn't get a pulse. He put them both in his boat and hauled it back to town. The doctor met them at the docks, but he pronounced Reece dead right there."

I shook my head. "No wonder Petey lost it. What a horrible thing."

"I think he might have been okay if his mother hadn't passed from cancer about six months before. He'd been a real trouper through her entire illness. The first and only time I saw him cry was at her funeral, but despite his brave front, I know it was a huge blow. Petey and Reece had been best friends since the crib. I don't think Petey was capable of handling two huge losses in such a short time."

"And one in such a horrific manner that he was witness to."

Ida Belle nodded. "Add to that the amount of time Petey was underwater and you have something doctors haven't been able to fix. I have never felt as bad for someone as I did for that boy and his father. Two lives were effectively lost that day. The Petey that remained was nothing like the boy before, and anyone who knows him knows good and well he's not capable of poaching."

I frowned, considering Ida Belle's words. "But given what happened, wouldn't Petey have more reason than most to hate alligators?"

"Sure, and I see where you're going with that, but there's one problem—Petey's scared to death of water now. He hasn't set foot in a boat or even on a dock ever since it happened. He won't even take a bath. Quincy had to convert Petey's bathtub to a walk-in shower. He had to wash him down outside with a hose until the construction was done. That boy won't so much as walk in a puddle."

"Then what in the world kind of evidence could the game warden have on him? Some of those lines we found couldn't have been baited from the bank. Betting on some of those limbs to hold an adult, especially that far out, would have been a huge risk for someone afraid of puddles."

"I know. That's what worries me."

"You think someone's setting him up?"

Ida Belle shook her head. "I don't want to think it, but I can't come up with any other logical answer."

"But who would do such a thing?"

"I have no idea." Ida Belle looked at me, her expression

grim. "I know we were investigating this poacher just to try out your detective legs, but things just got more serious. And personal. We've got to catch the poacher before the state puts that boy on trial based on trumped-up charges."

"We'll catch him. You have my word on that."

Chapter Nine

I had as much intention of going to the hospital to have my arm checked out as I did pressing charges against Quincy for assault. So after lunch, Ida Belle and I headed to my house to fill Gertie in on what had happened to Petey and Quincy. When we got there, Gertie was in the backyard, waving a package of Oreos at the bayou and calling for Godzilla.

"No luck?" I asked.

Gertie turned around and sighed. "Not so much as an air bubble."

"Maybe he's just hiding or sleeping off a casserole hangover," I said, trying to sound sincere, but in reality, I hoped Godzilla was far, far away from my backyard and wasn't planning on visiting anytime soon. If ever.

"You're probably right," Gertie said. "Maybe he'll come out this evening. What's wrong with you two? You both have this look like something bad happened. Was Francine out of food or something?"

"Let's head inside," I said. "It's hot as hell out here and you might need a drink once we tell you what's happening."

We headed inside into the air-conditioned kitchen, and Ida Belle poured us all a big glass of sweet tea.

"Well?" Gertie asked. "Out with it."

We filled Gertie in on everything that had happened with Quincy and Petey and my fake assault claim. Gertie listened without speaking until we were completely done, then after several seconds of complete silence, she exploded.

"What the hell is wrong with people?" She jumped up out of her chair and started pacing the kitchen. "That boy is no more capable than a small child. Besides, he's scared to death of the water now. He couldn't possibly have done this."

"We know," Ida Belle said. "I explained everything to Fortune, and trust me, no one here thinks Petey is the poacher, and I'm certain Carter doesn't either."

"Then why doesn't he tell the state to stick it up their butt?" Gertie asked.

"Because then Celia would have a sure reason to fire him," I said, "and if he loses his job, he can't help Petey at all."

My words seemed to mollify Gertie a little, but she still looked mad as heck.

"I know Carter's between a rock and a hard place," Gertie said, "and that he's just doing whatever he can to stay above water because otherwise, he's no help to nobody. But I swear, if I were him, I'd have already pulled a drive-by from here to the Gulf of Mexico."

I nodded. I'd started a hit list my first day in town, and Gertie had been working on hers a lot longer than me. It probably took up a ream of paper by now.

"What about Quincy?" I asked.

Ida Belle shrugged. "What about him?"

"Well, you all claim Petey couldn't be the poacher and based on what you're telling me about him, I agree. So if the state has enough evidence that they're requiring Carter to hold him, then that means someone must have set him up. I can't see anyone having that big a grudge against Petey, so what about Quincy?"

"That's a lot of risk and effort just to get back at someone you don't like," Ida Belle said.

"True," I said, "but we all know crazy doesn't lend itself to logic. Clearly, Petey is Quincy's weak spot, so someone trying to get to him would do it best by coming after Petey."

"That's downright evil," Gertie said, "but I see your point. The problem is, I can't think of why anyone would have a problem with Quincy. He's a computer programmer. Used to work in New Orleans, but ever since the accident, he works from home. He buys groceries once a week and other than that, I don't think he leaves the house unless it's for a doctor's appointment or he's looking for Petey, who likes to wander."

I frowned. It didn't sound like a good setup for creating an archenemy. "So no possibility of a fishing rival, someone who's butt-hurt over losing some local contest, or something equally silly to all of us sane people?"

Gertie shook her head. "I make it a point to go visit Quincy once a month. If I didn't, I probably wouldn't have seen him since Reece's funeral. I just can't see how he could make someone that angry sitting inside his house on a computer."

"Yeah," I agreed. "It doesn't sound like a promising angle, but I'm not quite ready to let it go. Is there anyone who is good friends with Quincy? Someone who might know more about his personal life than you do?"

"Ramona Barron," Gertie said. "She's Reece's mother."

"The boy who died?" I asked.

"Yeah," Gertie said. "She has dinner with Quincy and Petey every Sunday night. If anyone knows something about Quincy that the rest of us don't, it would be Ramona."

"Then maybe we should talk to Ramona," I said.

Gertie and Ida Belle looked at each other, and I got the impression that my suggestion wasn't going to meet with any heel clicking.

"Is there a problem with talking to Ramona?" I asked.

Ida Belle sighed. "She's not going to shoot at us if we pull up in her driveway or anything, but Ramona was always a hermit and an odd duck. No one knows who Reece's father was and as far as we know, there's never been a man around. Reece's funeral was the first time I'd seen her in five years or better, and I haven't seen her since. Walter delivers her groceries, and he says she leaves money on the porch."

"We can try," Gertie said, "but even if we manage to find her, there's no guarantee she'll talk to us."

"Life holds no guarantees, right?" I said. "But all the detective stuff I've been reading says the more you learn about the victim, the more likely you are to figure out the perpetrator. I can't talk to dead alligators, but now that Petey has been offered up as a sacrificial lamb, maybe finding out more about him and Quincy will give us another direction to move in."

"It certainly wouldn't hurt," Ida Belle agreed. "And it's not like we have anything else to go on."

Gertie nodded. "I'll try anything to get Petey back at home where he belongs. And we've still got the Swamp Bar tonight. That's two things that might give us something new."

I held in a sigh. It wasn't that I had forgotten about our Swamp Bar excursion. It was more that I'd intentionally blocked it until I couldn't any longer, which would probably be right around the time Gertie pulled whatever horror she had in mind for me to wear out of her huge handbag.

"Then let's get going," Ida Belle said. "I need to put another coat of wax on my new baby's bumper before we take it to the Swamp Bar tonight. I don't want bugs sticking to it."

Night bugs in Louisiana were more of the small reptile variety, and I didn't know of any wax in the world that would prevent them from sticking to a bumper, even with two coats, but I also knew better than to make suggestions to Ida Belle concerning her personal transportation. Besides, I was more concerned about myself sticking to the passenger's seat than how the bugs would fare.

We piled into my Jeep and headed for the highway. Ida Belle gave me directions that included Sinful classics such as 'turn off the paved road,' 'watch for stray cows,' and 'as long as this bridge holds, this is the shortest route.' Finally, we inched down a narrow dirt lane to a tiny house nestled in cypress trees.

The house itself surprised me a little. I guess I always pictured hermits living in some scary shack that you would expect to see in a horror movie, but this was a neat bungalow with fresh yellow paint and a row of flowers in front. On the front porch were several hanging plants and a rocking chair with a pillow. It was so inviting that it looked out of place in this dim, remote location.

"I hope she's here," Gertie said.

"I saw a curtain move as we pulled up," I said. "Someone's in there."

"One hurdle down," Ida Belle said. "If we can get her to answer the door and talk, we'll be killing it."

We walked up onto the porch, and Ida Belle knocked on the door. We waited for several seconds, listening for any sound of movement inside, but the house was eerily silent.

"She's pretending she's not here," Gertie whispered.

Ida Belle knocked again, and this time she called out. "Ramona. It's Ida Belle. It's important that I talk to you. It's about Quincy and Petey."

Gertie gave her an approving look. "If she doesn't answer for that, she won't for anything."

We heard footsteps inside, and several seconds later, the door inched open and a woman stared out at us.

Five foot three. One hundred sixty pounds. Wary expression. One arm hidden behind the door. Probably clutching a shotgun.

She stared at us for several uncomfortable seconds, then inclined her head toward me. "Who's she?"

"She's a friend of ours," Ida Belle said. "Marge Boudreaux's niece. You remember Marge?"

Ramona looked me up and down, then nodded. "Marge was really nice to me when Reece passed. I…still owe her for something."

I tried to hold in my excitement, but it looked as if we had a crack in the dam.

"Can we come in and talk to you?" Ida Belle asked.

"Are Quincy and Petey all right?" Ramona asked.

"Physically, yes," Ida Belle said, "but there's been some trouble and we're hoping you can help us sort it out."

"I don't know what I can possibly offer," Ramona said, "but if Quincy and Petey are in trouble, then I want to help any way I can." She pulled the door open and stood back so that we could enter.

The inside of the house matched the outside—both in stark comparison to the somewhat gloomy owner. The living room was painted a cheery blue, and original oil paintings of the swamp and shrimp boats hung on the walls. I stepped close to one and noticed the initials RB.

"Did you paint these?" I asked.

Ramona nodded. "I have an old friend who sells them for me in New Orleans. The money from the sales and the little bit my mother left me are what I get by on, but I don't need much."

"They're beautiful," I said. "You're very talented."

Ramona looked down at the floor, clearly embarrassed by the praise. "Please sit down," she said.

We all sat, and Ida Belle began to fill Ramona in on what

had happened with Petey. A flush crept up Ramona's face as Ida Belle talked, and her hands began to twitch. When Ida Belle finished, Ramona was silent for so long, I wondered if she'd processed everything she'd heard. Finally, she rose from her chair and shouted, "That's a bunch of horseshit!"

"We know it is," Gertie said, trying to calm down the clearly irate woman. "And Carter knows it is, but as long as the state says to hold Petey, he can't do anything about it without risking his job."

Ramona took deep breaths, shaking her head. Her chest heaved up and down with the effort. Finally, she sat back down. "It's that witch Celia. If she wasn't trying to get Carter fired, he could do his job the way he ought to be able to."

"That's true enough," Ida Belle said, "but even Carter couldn't go against the state."

"Maybe he would still have to hold Petey," Ramona said, "but he wouldn't have had any problem letting Quincy stay there before that devil was running Sinful." She looked over at me and nodded. "Thank you for seeing that Quincy got into jail. That was smart thinking."

I sighed. "What in the world are things coming to when the best thing you do in a day is getting someone thrown in jail?"

"That woman is the root of all evil," Ramona said. "I don't care what anyone thinks. I still say that the day she was put in charge of Sinful is the worst day in the town's history."

"You'll get no argument from me," Gertie said. "We're all praying the election audit gives us a different result."

"And if it doesn't?" Ramona asked. "Someone needs to do something about that woman."

I have to admit that I'd thought the same thing many, many times, but Ramona's intensity was a bit disconcerting. And even if Celia disappeared into a bright ball of light, that wouldn't solve the problem with Petey and Louisiana Wildlife and Fisheries.

"We have this theory," I said, "that if the state really has evidence against Petey, then it must have been planted."

"Of course it was planted!" Ramona said. "That boy isn't capable of poaching. He's barely capable of getting dressed anymore."

"But if it was planted," Ida Belle said, "then that means someone targeted Petey specifically."

Ramona frowned. "I hadn't thought of it that way. Why would someone do that?"

"We were hoping you might be able to help us with that question," Gertie said. "You probably know Quincy and Petey better than anyone else, so you would be aware of any problems they've had with other people...things that might give a less stable mind a reason to get revenge."

Ramona was silent for a while, her brow wrinkled in concentration, then she slowly shook her head. "I just can't think of anything. You know Quincy. He's the nicest man around and keeps to himself as much as possible. How do you create a enemy that determined when you rarely leave your house?"

I couldn't help feeling a bit disappointed. Ramona had the same opinion of Quincy that Gertie and Ida Belle had. Not that I was expecting her to jump up and shout out a name, but I guess I figured everyone had someone who was mad at them for some real or imagined slight.

"What about Petey?" I asked. "I know you all agree he couldn't hurt anyone, but Gertie said he liked to wander about. Could he have unintentionally caused a problem?"

"I talked to Quincy about Petey's wandering," Ramona said. "I saw him several times when I was checking rabbit traps. He would walk the trails from Sinful through the marsh and the woods and to the highway and back."

"But you never saw him near the water?" I asked.

Ramona frowned. "I was fishing about two months ago and saw Petey standing twenty feet or so from the bank. He was just staring at the water, not moving. I called out to him but he showed no sign that he heard or saw me. After a couple minutes, he turned around and walked back into the trees."

"That's weird," Gertie said. "He hasn't gone near the water since that day, far as I knew."

"Me too," Ramona agreed. "I told Quincy what I saw and he said he questioned Petey, but the boy refused to talk about it. Quincy dismissed it as an oddity, but then a month ago, I saw him doing the same thing again, except this time, he was closer to the bank…maybe ten feet away."

"Like he's working up the courage to get closer," I said.

"Maybe," Ramona said. "I just don't know."

Ida Belle shook her head. "It's strange, but I don't think it makes a difference. There's a huge gap between standing ten feet from the bank and getting in a boat, baiting hooks, and hauling in gators. Based on what Ramona saw, it took the boy a month to move ten feet."

Gertie nodded. "At that rate, it would take him a lifetime to get to the rest."

"Then we still circle back to someone having a problem with Petey," I said.

"But that doesn't make sense either," Ramona said. "I can't imagine anyone having a problem with Petey that they wouldn't take to Quincy. Everyone knows the boy and knows the situation. Even the less decent among us wouldn't do such a thing to that family. And to what end? Even if that trumped-up evidence sticks, Petey isn't competent to stand trial. He'd be released back to his dad and everything would be just as it was before."

And then something new occurred to me. "What if Petey saw something?"

"Something that someone else didn't want him to see?" Gertie asked.

"Of course, something they didn't want seen," Ida Belle said. She looked over at me, nodding. "So if they wanted Petey out of the way, and discredited, the easiest way to do it would be to set him up."

"But what did he see?" Gertie asked.

"Maybe the poacher," I said. "That would make the most sense. The guy frames him for what he was doing, figuring if Petey points the finger at him, no one will believe him since Petey was the one with the evidence against him."

"And with Petey's issues, the court probably wouldn't believe him, and that's assuming we could get him to talk in the first place." She banged her hand on the chair. "Damn it! I bet you're right."

"So how do we get Petey to talk?" I asked.

"If Petey knows something," Gertie said, "Quincy is the only person who might be able to get it out of him."

"Then we need to talk to Quincy," I said.

Ida Belle nodded and we all rose. "Thank you, Ramona, for speaking to us."

"If there's something I can do," Ramona said, "anything at all, you let me know."

I had a feeling from her tone that Ramona really meant the "anything" part of her offer, which was both heartening and somewhat scary.

I started to walk out, but then something Ramona said earlier came back to me, and I couldn't stop from asking. "You said earlier that you owed Marge for something. Do you mind telling me what it was? I don't want to collect or anything. I was just curious."

"Since she was your aunt and you're helping Petey and Quincy, I'll tell you. But you have to keep her secret. I've never told anyone else before now and won't again."

"I won't say a word," I assured her.

Ramona nodded. "Marge killed the gator. The one that got Reece."

We all stared. Of all the things I might have guessed, and I'd manufactured some good ones during our conversation, that was one I wouldn't have come up with.

"The gator?" Gertie asked.

Ramona nodded.

I knew it was probably a bad thing to ask, but my curiosity refused to be pushed aside. "How do you know it was the right one? I mean, there's so many of them."

Ramona walked over to a hutch just to my right and opened it. She removed something from inside, then turned around and handed it to me. I took the glass jar full of liquid from her, wondering where the hell this was going, when I realized the thing suspended in liquid was a finger.

"Holy crap!" I stared up at her. "Is this…?"

"Reece lost a finger in the attack," Ramona said. "Marge gutted the gator and found it inside. That's how I'm certain it was the right gator. I preserved it in pickling juice. Keeps the bacteria out."

I handed the jar back to Ramona, slightly perturbed by the fact that I was holding a dead boy's pickled finger kept in a hutch in his mother's living room.

"Not to beat a dead horse or anything," I said, "but how can you be sure it's his finger? There's a few missing round here."

"That's true enough," Ramona said, "but this one belonged

to a young person, and Reece had a scar on that finger where he'd jammed a fishing hook through it the year before. You can still see the scar."

"Wow," Gertie said. "That's really something. Marge never said a word to us."

"I don't think she wanted anyone to know," Ramona said. "I doubt she got her on her first try. Who knows how many she killed to find the right one. She wouldn't have wanted anyone else to be implicated if she was caught."

"That's definitely Marge," Ida Belle said.

Ramona looked at me. "Your aunt was different. A lot of people thought her strange, but she had a big heart and a huge desire to make things right. She might not have shouted it from the rooftops, but she was always there, behind the scenes."

Gertie nodded and sniffed. "Marge was one of a kind."

"Thank you for telling me that," I said, feeling disappointed that Marge wasn't really my aunt and that I'd never gotten to meet her. I'm certain I would have liked her.

"I'm glad I got the opportunity," Ramona said. "What Marge did changed things for me. I stopped living the day Reece died. I know most people would say I never have lived, but they don't know me. I like my solitude. I have my work and my interests and they keep me busy during waking hours. But after my boy was gone, nothing mattered to me any longer. Not until Marge brought me that finger. I know some would find it macabre, but it breathed life back into me. So for that, I am forever grateful to her."

"I glad she could help," I said. "And I'm really sorry about Reece."

Ramona straightened a bit and nodded. "I'll fix some food and take it down to the sheriff's department. I assume Carter can still let them eat."

"Celia hasn't insisted he starve the prisoners," Ida Belle said.

"Yet," Gertie said.

"Thank you again for talking to us," Ida Belle said. "We best get back to Sinful and have a chat with Quincy and Petey."

We headed back out to my Jeep, and I set off back to Sinful. "Okay, does anyone else thinks it's sorta creepy that Ramona has her dead son's finger in her living room?"

"Totally."

"No doubt."

Ida Belle and Gertie both answered at once.

"I mean, I get it," I said. "Sorta. But I think once I verified it was the right finger, I would have buried it or something."

"Me too," Gertie said, "but Ramona has always been eccentric. If it works for her, then I don't suppose it's doing any harm. Not many people have ever crossed her doorstep, and she's not likely to show anyone else besides us."

Ida Belle shook her head. "I still can't believe Marge did that without telling us. We would have helped."

"She didn't want you to get in trouble," I said.

Ida Belle raised one eyebrow. "Have you forgotten who you're talking to? We invented trouble."

I laughed. "Okay. Then maybe she didn't want you in more trouble."

"That's probably true," Ida Belle said. "And it's not like this is the first time we've found out Marge kept secrets from us." Ida Belle sighed. "I wonder sometimes if we ever truly know someone."

"You know me," Gertie said. "I'm an open book."

"Really?" Ida Belle asked. "Then tell me what you've got in that Pandora's box of a purse you carry."

"I could tell you," Gertie said. "But then I'd have to kill

you."

"There's probably ten things or better in that purse that could handle the job," I said.

"I suppose I know you well enough," Ida Belle said to Gertie. "And I suppose everyone has something they're keeping to themselves. We're all human, after all."

"Except Celia," Gertie said.

I glanced over at Ida Belle and watched as her smile faded into a pensive look. I wondered what secrets she kept to herself. With Gertie, I believed it was mostly what you see is what you get, but Ida Belle ran deeper. Under that calm resolve was something unspoken.

But then, she could say the same about me.

Chapter Ten

I pulled into Sinful, planning to park in front of the sheriff's department and charm Carter into letting us see Quincy and Petey, but those plans went out the window when I saw Celia standing on the sidewalk, glaring at me.

"This can't be good," I said.

I parked farther down in front of the General Store and as we climbed out, Celia came stomping over toward us. Her face was red, and in the bright pink dress with huge yellow flowers, she looked like a really tacky overstuffed chair.

"What kind of nonsense are you up to now?" Celia asked. "I know Quincy didn't assault you. Carter thinks he can fool me, but he can't."

"Carter had nothing to do with it," I said, and pointed to the red marks on my arm. "Quincy grabbed me. The proof is right there."

Celia narrowed her eyes. "Oh, I have no doubt that a lot of people would like to grab you and shake you until you left town, but I know you're up to something."

"The only thing I'm up to is shopping," I said. "And you're in my way."

"If Quincy really assaulted you," Celia said, "how come you haven't filed a report yet? I asked Carter and he said you would file it after you'd seen a doctor. He's in the office now. It wouldn't take a minute to get your statement in writing. Then you could be certain that woman-beater Quincy and his criminal son wouldn't be walking around Sinful."

If I gave Carter a statement, Celia would see to it that Quincy sat in jail until he went to trial. A trial that I would have to testify at, starting with stating my name with my hand on a Bible. Not a good look for someone whose entire identity was a lie. And even if there weren't that tiny problem with lying under oath, I didn't want Quincy in jail any longer than he had to be.

"The doctor said I needed to ice my arm, take some aspirin, and rest," I said, "which is what I'm going to do as soon as you stop your yapping and let me go buy some aspirin. I'll file the report when I feel better. I doubt Quincy is a flight risk."

"You may pretend to be all injured innocence," Celia said, "but I don't buy it for a minute. Whatever you're up to, you're going down for it this time."

"You better hurry up," Gertie said. "The election recount results will be in soon."

Celia glared at her. "And when they proclaim me the winner—again—things are going to change around here. The days of you two running this town are over."

"You may get to be mayor of this town," Ida Belle said, "but you will never matter."

Celia's eyes widened and she sputtered for a moment. Apparently unable to think of a witty comeback, she whirled around and stalked off down the sidewalk, then plopped down on a bench in front of the sheriff's department.

"Well, I guess strolling in the sheriff's department and nicely asking questions is out," I said.

"With the demon queen sitting there, people will be afraid to go in or out," Gertie said. "What do we do now?"

"We go into the store," I said, "like we were pretending to do in the first place, and have a chat with Walter. Maybe Carter told him something. We can regroup there."

We went inside the store and loitered between the aisles while Walter finished up with a customer, then headed for the register when the store was empty. Walter frowned when he saw us coming.

"I got word that you heard about Petey," he said. "Carter called earlier and had me bring a couple sleeping bags and pillows down there for Quincy and the boy."

"Heard about it and already working on it," I said.

"Good," Walter said. "Setting that boy up for poaching is downright evil."

"So you think someone set him up too?" I asked.

"What the heck else could it have been?" Walter asked. "That boy didn't kill those gators, so whoever put those lines, hooks, bait, and alligator skins in his boat couldn't have had anything else in mind."

I looked over at Ida Belle and Gertie, who both looked worried. No wonder the state told Carter he had to hold Petey. The evidence was definitely tilted in the wrong direction.

Walter looked back and forth among us, probably wondering why we hadn't spoken yet. "You didn't know about the evidence, did you? Well, crap. I've gone and repeated police business that I shouldn't have."

"Don't look at it as breaking a confidence," Gertie said. "Look at it as saving us from having to break and enter to get a peek at Carter's files."

Walter gave her a pained look. "Please don't give me details. Just having a good idea what you are up to is enough to get me in hot water with Carter for not telling."

"You let the horses out of the barn," Gertie said. "Don't be getting all self-righteous with us now."

"She's right," Ida Belle said. "Might as well finish up what you started."

Walter looked torn, so I jumped in. "Look, all we want is to get Petey cleared. We can do that a lot faster if we can disprove the evidence against him, which would be a heck of a lot easier if we knew what that evidence was. We were going to ask Carter—or, as Gertie said, steal it if necessary. But with Celia Arceneaux sitting guard in front of the sheriff's department, we can't get in to talk to anyone."

Walter stiffened. "Celia is sitting in front of the sheriff's department?"

Gertie nodded. "Her fat butt is plopped on the bench right outside the door."

Walter banged his hand on the counter, and we all started. He was usually so calm, but right now he looked mad enough to spit. "What the hell is that woman trying to do? She's tearing this town apart with her hate. And to what end?"

"To get to me," Ida Belle said quietly.

Walter let out a sigh and shook his head. "I will never understand a desire for a reckoning so strong that you burn down your own house to get it, but that's exactly what Celia seems determined to do."

"Then help us win," I said. "Tell us what you know. It's either that or we break in the back door of the sheriff's department and wait for Carter to leave his desk. It's not optimal."

"I'm afraid what I know isn't good," Walter said. "I told you the gear for hunting alligator was found in Petey's boat. His fingerprints were on it, and when the game warden picked him up, he said Petey was walking in circles, mumbling incoherently, and had blood on his shirt that matched blood on the piece of tail in the boat."

I frowned, completely confused. "Why does Petey even

have a boat?"

"He had it before the accident," Gertie said. "Quincy never got rid of it. I think he felt like doing that meant he was admitting Petey was never going to get better."

My chest tightened a little at Quincy's dilemma. "Where was the boat kept?"

"As far as I know," Gertie said, "he never moved it from JC's."

I waited for the rest of the explanation, but apparently, Gertie thought she was done.

"JC Hammond owns a little stretch of dirt with a boat ramp," Ida Belle explained. "Several locals pay him a small amount to keep their boats there. Mostly those that live in the neighborhood and don't want to clog up their driveways."

"I assume, since I've never seen it, that this stretch of dirt is remote?" I asked.

Ida Belle nodded. "It's a couple miles outside of town, but JC's place is the only thing down the road."

"So no reason to go there other than for the boat," I said, then I looked up at Walter. "Why was the game warden there digging through boats, anyway? And is that even legal?"

"All a game warden needs is suspicion of illegal activity and he can search a car, boat, house, whatever," Walter said.

I perked up. "Really? That sounds like the perfect job for me—not having to get permission for anything."

Walter nodded. "There is some truth to that."

"So why was the game warden checking Petey's boat?" Ida Belle asked.

"He claimed it was an anonymous tip," Walter said.

I rolled my eyes. "I bet. The poacher heard that Carter was investigating, so he planted that stuff in Petey's boat, then called it in himself."

Ida Belle frowned. "I'm sure you're right, but it doesn't explain how the blood from the boat got on Petey."

"Maybe he was in the boat," Gertie said. "It's not in the water, and with Ramona seeing him standing near the bank…I don't know, maybe he's trying to return to the way things used to be."

I nodded. "Then he found the stuff in there, touched it, not understanding why it was in his boat, then freaked out a little when he found the gator tail, which would explain the acting incoherently and mumbling."

"We ought to check out the boat," Gertie said.

"I'm sure the state confiscated it," Ida Belle said. "What we really need to do is talk to Petey. If he knows who the poacher is, we can figure out a way to get proof."

"Wait a minute," Walter said. "You think Petey knows who the poacher is? And what's all this about Ramona saying he's standing near the bank?"

We filled Walter in on our visit with Ramona and our theory that the reason Petey was being set up was because he'd seen the poacher during his wanderings.

When we were done, Walter blew out a breath. "I've been racking my brains trying to figure out why anyone would want to harm that boy. I bet you've hit on it. But what kind of person does that to someone like Petey?"

"A desperate, despicable one," Gertie said.

"And arrogant," Ida Belle said. "I'm sure he thinks no one will question the evidence."

"To hell with Celia," I said. "Let's just go in the back door. I'll call Carter and tell him to let us in. We won't even have to pick a lock. Do it all aboveboard. More or less."

I pulled out my cell phone and dialed him up. He answered on the first ring.

"Gertie would like to get in to see Petey and Quincy," I said. "She's worried."

I wasn't about to tell Carter the truth. If he knew we were butting into his investigation, he'd clear out the drunks and lock us up until he caught the poacher. And with Celia tying his hands at every opportunity, that could be a long visit on a hard cot. But Gertie was family and if we could at least get her in, we could coach her through the questions by phone.

"Even if I wanted to let her in here, I can't," Carter said. "Celia is parked outside my front door and she's got one of her minions parked outside the back. Unless she can teleport, no one gets in unless it's official police business."

"Can't you shoot Celia?" I asked. "It would be a community service."

He let out a single laugh. "Don't tempt me. Sorry, but I can't help Gertie. Tell her they're fine, and I'll go ask Quincy if he needs her to handle anything at his house while he's here."

"Okay. Thanks for that."

I hung up the phone and filled them in.

"I guess Carter said no to your shooting request?" Gertie asked.

"Maybe next time," I said.

"I could get one of you in," Walter said. "But getting out would be a problem."

I perked up. I'd gotten out of some of the deadliest places in the world, and that didn't even include the Swamp Bar.

"Getting out of the building isn't the problem," I said. "And once I'm outside the building, they'd have to catch me."

"My money is on Fortune in a footrace," Gertie said. "We've been eating banana pudding on Sundays ever since she got here."

"And if it's Carter who's chasing her?" Ida Belle pointed

out.

"She's been eluding Carter since she got here as well," Gertie said. "My money's still on Fortune."

"Exactly how would you get me inside?" I asked.

"Let me show you," he said, and waved us to the door of the stockroom. Once inside, he pointed to a medium-sized wooden crate. "It's small, but you'd fit in it okay. I can pretend to be making a delivery to Carter and drop you off right in the break room. Given that Quincy and Petey are in the storeroom, that's probably where he'd have me leave it."

"Wouldn't Carter know whether or not he's ordered supplies?" Ida Belle said.

"Maybe," Walter said, "but he's distracted right now, and even if he thought my old mind had screwed up, he wouldn't take time out from the rest of what he's got going on to set me straight."

Gertie pulled the top off the crate and peered inside. "I could fit in here."

"If we folded you in half," Ida Belle said. "But then you'd never get out, and Walter might not be able to stick around to help. It's not like jumping out of a birthday cake. Fortune will have to push the top off that crate and then do some serious yoga to get out of there."

"Besides," I added, "Quincy and Petey are in the storeroom, which I figure Carter has locked. So the only way in is through the ceiling."

"What's the smallest space you've ever been in?" Gertie asked me.

"Culvert, air ventilation system, steamer trunk, and once, an oven."

All three of them stared at me.

"You win," Gertie said, "and when we have time, I want to

hear the oven story."

Walter tipped the crate over and dumped a bunch of shredded paper out, leaving a bit of a cushion in the bottom. "That should help the body parts a little," he said.

I nodded. "And with sound deadening."

He tilted the crate back up and I climbed in, tucked myself into fetal position, arms up so that I could break off the top when the time came. Walter slid the top of the crate on and looked down at me before the last sliver of light disappeared.

"You sure you're okay in there?" he asked.

"This is the most rest I've gotten all day."

He grinned and slid the top in place. I heard him tapping the corners, probably securing the top with small nails, then the crate tilted to one side and I heard the squeaking wheels of a dolly as he slid it underneath.

"You two mind the store while I'm gone," Walter said as he rolled me out of the stockroom.

"See if you can get anything else out of Carter while you're there," Ida Belle said.

"And try to run over Celia's foot with the dolly," Gertie said.

I heard the bells from the front door jangle and the crate bumped along a bit, then stopped and went level. Then I heard Celia.

"Where do you think you're going with that?" she asked.

"I'm going about my business," Walter said, "and I suggest you do the same."

"Do you have a copy of the order for this delivery?" Celia asked.

"No, but I'll tell you what I do have—limited patience. If you don't get out of my way, I'm running right over those ugly shoes with this dolly. When you fall down, I might go to work on the other end."

I bit my lip to keep myself from laughing. Celia must have decided she didn't have a leg to stand on, or she was afraid of losing the leg to Walter's dolly. Either way, we started bumping again, then I heard a door open.

Walter called out. "Got that supply delivery for you."

"I don't remember an order," Carter said.

"Then it's a good thing you've got me to," Walter said. "Hold that door open so I can bring this in."

"Let me get it," Carter said.

"No need," Walter said. "It's not heavy. Just bulky."

"Must be paper products," Carter said, "but I swear I stocked up on paper towels and toilet paper a couple weeks ago."

"So?" Walter said. "Not like it's going to go to waste. Well, technically, I guess some of it will go to waste." He laughed. "I'll leave it in the break room."

"That's fine. Can you manage the door? I've got a situation I'm trying to deal with."

"I saw your situation. If I'd been carting something heavier, I might have accidentally bumped into her."

"No use punishing a perfectly good crate," Carter said. "Thanks, Walter."

The bumping ceased and the crate began to glide. Based on the number of turns we'd made, I figured we were in the hallway going toward the break room. We stopped again and I heard a door open, then the crate moved once more then went flat. I heard a muffled yell and strained, trying to make out what was going on.

"That's Carter calling for me," Walter said. "I was hoping to help you out of there."

"Go," I said. "I've got this."

I heard the break room door open and close again, then

waited and listened to make sure no one else was nearby. As certain as I was ever going to be, I thrust myself up, pushing the top off the crate with my forearms. It flew straight up in the air. I popped up and grabbed it as it began to descend, then sat it quietly next to the crate as I climbed out. I took a couple seconds to position the top back in place, pushing the finishing nails back into the original holes, then crept to the door and opened it a crack.

The hallway was empty, and I couldn't hear anyone talking. Either Walter had left the building, or they were being very quiet. I didn't think the second option likely. Walter would find a reason to make noise just for my benefit. I slipped out of the break room and hurried to the storeroom to try the door, but it was locked, just as I'd suspected.

I didn't want to risk checking the front office to see if Carter was there, so I went back into the break room and climbed on top of the kitchen counter, then pushed one of the ceiling tiles to the side. I jumped up and grabbed the wall, pulling myself up onto the rafters, then slid the tile back in place. I crawled along the rafter until I got to where I thought the storeroom would be and lifted one of the ceiling tiles.

I saw Quincy sitting in a chair off to my left, a young man sitting on the floor beside him. I pushed the tile to the side and stuck my head out of the ceiling.

"Quincy," I said in a loud whisper.

Quincy looked back and forth around the room.

"Up here," I said.

He glanced up, and his eyes widened when he saw me.

"What in the world are you doing up there?" he asked.

"It's a long story, but I need to talk to Petey. I'm coming down."

I pushed the panel all the way over, then lay across the

rafter and flipped over it into the storeroom, dropping onto a table in the middle of the room. Petey jumped up from the floor and pointed. He was starting to yell when Quincy put his hand over the boy's mouth.

"She's a friend, Petey," Quincy said as he slowly removed his hand from Petey's mouth. "Don't be scared."

Petey stared at me for a while, then looked up at the ceiling. "Angel," he whispered.

It took me a minute to realize he thought I was an angel because I'd come from above.

"Sort of," Quincy said, and smiled.

"That's probably the first and last time someone calls me that," I said.

"That was some kind of move," Quincy said.

"I was a gymnast when I was young."

Quincy still looked confused but appeared too stressed to focus on the strangeness of the situation. "You said you needed to talk to Petey?" he asked.

"Yes. We tried to get in here the regular way, but Celia and her minions are blocking access to the sheriff's department, so I had to sneak in. But that's not important. Let me tell you what we've found out."

I filled him in on our talk with Ramona, what Walter told us about the evidence, and our theory that Petey had seen the poacher.

Quincy ran one hand over his head and plopped back down in the chair. "It's all so fantastic, but at the same time, it's the only thing that makes sense. My God, what if he'd simply decided to…" Quincy looked over at Petey, then back at me. "Instead of…"

I nodded. The poacher was taking a risk leaving an eyewitness, but then Petey wouldn't necessarily be considered reliable, and murder was a way bigger deal than poaching. It would take someone seriously deranged or someone who was certain they'd get away with it to kill Petey. Still, Quincy had a point. It wasn't like deranged hadn't paid a visit to Sinful a time or two before, and the criminal element had a tendency to react first and think about it later or not at all.

Quincy leaned over to look at Petey, who'd sunk back down into a squatting position on the sleeping bag. "Did you see someone in the bayou hurting alligators?"

Petey's eyes widened and he shook his head. Quincy looked up at me and mouthed, "He's lying."

I nodded. I didn't have to be Petey's parent to see that he was scared.

"If you saw someone hurt the alligators," Quincy said, "I need you to tell me. They can't hurt you, Petey. I won't let them."

Petey shook his head and waved his hands around the room.

"He thinks the bad guy put him in here," Quincy said.

It wasn't exactly untrue. It just wasn't true in the way Petey imagined it.

Quincy put his hands on Petey's shoulders. "We are here because the police think you hurt the alligators. Do you understand?"

"No!" Petey cried out.

"I know you didn't do it," Quincy said, "but the police think you did. If you tell the police who did it, they'll let you out of here and go find the bad guy."

Quincy glanced back at me when he said that last sentence, and I could tell that it killed him to tell his son that half-truth, but if we could get a name out of him, then hopefully, it wouldn't be hard to prove.

Petey stared at Quincy for a bit, and I started to think he was going to offer up a name, but then he shook his head and looked down at the floor. "Alligators bad."

Quincy sighed and looked up at me. "He thinks the poacher is doing a good thing."

Petey tucked his legs up to his chest, wrapped his arms around them, and started humming.

"He won't talk anymore," Quincy said. "Not when he's like this. He goes somewhere else when he's like this."

"But you think he saw something?"

"It's the only thing that makes sense. I'll keep trying to get it out of him. If we weren't locked up in this place, it would be easier, but with him already on edge...he's a lot harder to reach when he's this way."

"Quincy!" Carter's voice sounded outside the door. "I heard someone yell. You guys all right in there?"

Chapter Eleven

I heard a key rattling in the storeroom door and leaped from my sitting position on the table over a stack of paper boxes and did a roll into a shelf. I jumped up and steadied the shelf before it fell, then tucked myself behind the boxes just as the door opened and Carter stepped inside. I peered through a crack in between the boxes, praying that Carter didn't need copy paper.

"You all right?" Carter asked.

"Yes, we're fine," Quincy said. "Something startled him, I think."

"Angel!" Petey shouted, then went back to humming.

Quincy gave Carter an apologetic shrug. "I'm not sure what he's thinking. This isn't exactly the best place for him."

"If there was any other way…" Carter said.

"I know you're doing everything you can, but do you have any idea when the state is going to do something? They can't just leave him sitting here forever."

"I've called them four times already today but they keep stonewalling me. As soon as I know something, I'll be in here sharing it. The drunks should be out of the jail by this evening. If you're still here, we'll move you guys down there. It's not the Ritz, but at least there are beds and a toilet."

"I'm sure we'll manage, whatever the circumstances," Quincy said.

"Gertie wanted to talk to you and see if she could visit, but

I have Celia sitting out in front of the sheriff's department, so I can't let her in. Is there anything you need?"

"We need plenty," Quincy said, "but I'm afraid it's nothing you or Gertie can give us."

Carter nodded, looking defeated. I felt my chest constrict, and the overwhelming urge to burst out from behind the boxes and hug him came over me. Then common sense took hold again and I was back in spy mode.

"Okay," Carter said. "Call for me or bang on the door if you need something. Ally said Francine is providing dinner for you two."

"She outdid herself with lunch," Quincy said. "The good people in this town are why I stay. They still outweigh the bad."

"Yeah, they do." Carter left the storeroom, and I heard the door lock behind him.

I popped up from behind the boxes and climbed onto the table. "I have to run. Keep trying to get Petey to talk."

"I'll try, but I don't know how much good it will do if he's frightened."

"I'm working on an idea about that," I said. "I'll get back with you."

Quincy watched as I slid the ceiling tile back. "Do you need help? I can put a chair up there or give you a push."

"I'm good," I said, and leaped up, grabbing the rafter. I pulled myself up onto it and looked back down. Petey had risen from the floor and was pointing up at me.

"Angel," he said.

Quincy shook his head. "You're no angel, but darn if you seem completely human."

"There's probably some truth to that."

I slid the tile back in place and thought about my options. The back door wouldn't work because of the Celia contingent, nor could I risk walking all the way down the hall to get to it. The break room didn't have an exterior window, so that was out. My best choice was Carter's office on the back side of the building, but the window was clearly visible from the back door steps, where Celia's minion was perched.

What I needed was a distraction.

Then I remembered a pack of lunch meat sitting on the counter in the break room. If I could snag that meat, and with a little help from Ida Belle and Gertie, I just might be able to make it work.

If not, I'd stroll up front, get arrested for breaking into the sheriff's department, and the storeroom would get rather crowded.

Ten minutes later, I opened the window in Carter's office and peeked outside. I recognized Celia's cousin and right-hand man, Dorothy, sitting on the steps, crocheting something in a hideous orange color. I balled up some of the lunch meat and started tossing it out the window, first off to the right, then slowly leading toward the steps.

A couple minutes later, I heard Ida Belle call out and watched as she walked up to the steps. Dorothy immediately stiffened, clearly preparing for battle, but Ida Belle casually chatted until her shoulders relaxed a bit. Then she pointed toward the bayou and when Dorothy's back was turned, Ida Belle dropped something into the crochet bag.

Now all we needed was for Gertie to get Buddy Riker's hound dogs loose and the show would be on. I could hear them barking in the distance and figured Gertie must be near the pen. The sound wasn't moving yet, though, so they weren't out. I hoped Gertie had laid the trail to the edge of the tree line. The first piece of lunch meat I'd thrown had landed about ten feet from the edge of the trees. It was plenty close for a pair of hunting hounds to get a whiff of.

The barking increased in intensity, and then it started getting louder. They were headed this way. I watched at the edge of the tree line, waiting for them to burst out of the trees, but instead of dogs, Gertie barreled out of the brush, running like a madwoman with a string of hot links trailing behind her.

The dogs were right on her tail, grabbing at the flopping wieners. By the time she reached the window, the links were long gone, but Gertie kept right on running past the sheriff's department and around the corner.

Dorothy jumped up from the steps and both she and Ida Belle watched as Gertie huffed by them, then turned back around to eye the baying hounds. The dogs stopped running and went silent, sniffing the air. That was it! They'd caught scent of the lunch meat.

The dogs started baying and scurried down the invisible line of lunch meat I'd created, lifting the pieces from the grass as they barreled past. Dorothy was so intent on watching the dogs, she didn't see Ida Belle sneak off. The dogs picked up speed, trying to beat each other to the next prize. Dorothy stood like a statue on the bottom of the steps and began to look worried as the hounds drew closer.

Then the last bit of lunch meat was gone; the dogs stopped again, sniffing the air.

"Go on," Dorothy said as she lifted her crochet bag and swung it in front of her. "Shoo!"

I clamped one hand over my mouth to keep from laughing. She couldn't possibly have picked a worse move.

The dogs caught a whiff of whatever Ida Belle had dropped inside her bag and launched. One of them grabbed the bag midair and brought it down to the ground, ripping it from Dorothy's grasp. The other dog lunged for the prized bag and the first dog took off with it. When he launched, the hideous orange thing Dorothy had been making wrapped around her ankle, the other end securely fastened in the running dog's mouth. Her legs flew out from under her and she crashed onto the ground, screaming like a banshee. The second dog ran right over her head, still trying to get to the bag.

On the one hand, it was hilarious, and fell short of what Celia and her crew deserved, but it was also too much distraction. I'd wanted the dogs to scare Dorothy off, not tackle her. A second later, the back door to the sheriff's department flew open and Carter ran outside. He stopped short, probably trying to figure out why Dorothy and two dogs appeared to be launched in a tug-of-war battle over a crocheted something-or-other, but finally zeroed in on the problem and jumped in, trying to unwrap the fabric from Dorothy's ankle.

Just when I thought things couldn't get more entertaining, Celia showed up. She rounded the corner of the building as Carter pulled the fabric free from Dorothy's leg. He flung it backward, hitting Celia square in the face. The dogs, still on the trail of whatever goody Ida Belle had put in the bag, ran for the orange thing and both jumped at the same time, knocking Celia over backward, crocheting on top of her.

The first dog grabbed one end of the orange thing and took off. The second dog grabbed the other end of it and got a good mouthful of Celia's skirt along with it. When he took off, the skirt ripped all the way up to the waistband, leaving Celia showing all of her left leg and way too much of some other parts.

Since everyone I was trying to avoid was out back, and once again, I'd seen more of Celia than anyone ever wanted to, I took the opportunity to run down the hall and out the front door.

Myrtle, the dispatcher and a friend of Ida Belle's and Gertie's, just waved and didn't even bother to ask a question. I took a hard right as soon as I exited the building and almost ran smack into Ida Belle.

"Hurry up!" she said, motioning me toward the General Store.

"I *was* hurrying until you got in the way," I said as we took off down the sidewalk.

Gertie was sitting on Walter's seat behind the cash register, wheezing. Walter opened a bottle of water and handed it to her. She took a drink, coughed, and sprayed water all over Walter. He sighed and reached for a roll of paper towels on a display near the counter.

"Are you all right?" I asked Gertie.

She nodded. "Those dogs are faster than I thought they'd be."

"You weren't supposed to try to outrun them," I said. "You were supposed to leave the trail out of the woods before you turned them loose."

Gertie stared at me several seconds. "That probably would have been easier."

Ida Belle looked up at the ceiling, probably praying again.

"Did anyone see you get out?" Walter asked.

I nodded. "Myrtle."

"How in the world did Myrtle see you?" Walter asked. "She's supposed to be at the front desk."

"She was," I said. "When all hell broke loose, everyone ran to the back, so I left through the front door. Not like Myrtle is going to say anything."

"Myrtle won't even ask why you were there," Ida Belle says. "She knows the value of existing with little information."

Walter shook his head. "You are truly something. So what

was happening out back that everyone went running to?"

I filled them in on the attack of the hungry hound dogs, and by the time I got to the part about Celia's skirt, they were all laughing so hard they were crying.

Gertie was coughing so violently, Ida Belle started banging on her back. She drank some more water, then started to chant, "You saw London, you saw France, you saw Celia's underpants."

"Don't remind me," I said.

"At least she wears them," Ida Belle said.

I groaned. "Thank you for that visual."

Walter grimaced. "So was all this worth it?"

"Yes and no," I said, and described my conversation with Petey. "I'm sure Petey saw the poacher, but he's too scared to tell who it is. Quincy's going to keep working on him, but I had another idea. When I asked Petey about the poacher, his reaction was instant. He shook his head but it was clear that he was lying."

Gertie nodded. "He can't act at all. Whatever he's feeling comes out in his actions and expressions."

"Exactly," I said, "so I figured if we had some pictures of people we suspected of being the poacher, then he would react to a picture of the guilty party if we asked him if they were the bad guy."

"That's smart," Ida Belle said. "Unfortunately, our suspect list is currently lacking."

"But we're going to the Swamp Bar tonight," Gertie said. "I bet we can find all kinds of suspects there."

"True," Ida Belle said. "The trick, however, is getting pictures of them without someone getting suspicious or the potential guilty party noticing. Not everyone who frequents the Swamp Bar is single, and there's more than a few Baptists in there, including a couple of deacons. None of them would want a picture taken."

"We just have to be discreet," I said. "Practically everyone walks around looking at a cell phone these days. Just act like you're checking email or something. Not like anyone could hear a camera click with the racket in that place."

"Discreet," Ida Belle repeated. "Which leaves Gertie out."

"I can be discreet," Gertie argued.

"You haven't been discreet your entire life," Ida Belle said. "Even in the crib, you'd yank off your diaper and stroll around like it was perfectly fine."

"She makes a point," I said.

"Two against one again," Gertie pouted.

"I don't know anything about your toddler streaking adventures, and don't want to," I said, "but if we want to get pictures without drawing attention to ourselves, that means no outlandish getups. No hookers or nuns or whatever else you've got cooked up for dress tonight."

"Hookers and nuns?" Walter asked.

"Old news," I said.

"She doesn't want to talk about it because it worked," Gertie said.

"Everything works as long as you can outrun people," I said. "But for once, I'd like to walk into that bar and leave without threats, gunfire, explosion, or a boat, motorcycle, or car chase."

"Just how many times have you been to that bar?" Walter asked.

"Do you really want to know?" I asked.

He shook his head. "In rethinking my position, never mind."

"The lack of a car chase would be disappointing," Ida Belle said.

I stared. "I'm so sorry that you might not get the opportunity to scare us all to death in that bolt of lightning SUV you bought."

Ida Belle shrugged. "Sooner or later, you're going to be thanking God I bought that truck."

I cringed a bit because deep down in the pit of my stomach, I knew she was right. But that didn't mean I was going to jump up and down about it until it happened.

"So what are we supposed to do?" Gertie asked. "Walk in there like church ladies from Sinful?"

"When have I ever looked like a church lady?" Ida Belle asked.

"At church," Gertie replied.

"I think jeans, T-shirts, and tennis shoes all the way around are fine," I said. "Makeup that's a little too dark. Maybe some teased hair. That should work, and it's easy to put together."

"And to run in," Ida Belle said.

"I'm really trying to avoid running again," Gertie said.

Ida Belle nodded. "Then remember that tonight."

Chapter Twelve

Carter texted me late that evening asking if he could drop by for an hour or so. I figured that translated to, he was going to have to work that night, was hungry, and didn't have anything at his house to eat. Between Ally and Gertie, I was usually stocked with something good, and worst case, I could fix up a decent sandwich and throw in some cookies and a couple of beers.

I walked outside to let Gertie know that Carter was on his way. As soon as we had returned from my jailbreaking escapade and Gertie's running of the dogs, she'd headed out back to the bayou. She'd been out there ever since, waving a bag of cookies at the water and calling for Godzilla. So far, I'd lucked out and he hadn't made an appearance. I hoped that streak continued for our trip to the Swamp Bar.

"I'll give you two lovebirds some alone time," Gertie said. "I'll go home and pack clothes and supplies for tonight."

I had a brief flicker of fear over the word "supplies." I hoped she meant a toothbrush and whatever else she needed to stay the night, but I had a feeling the supplies she spoke of were for our Swamp Bar excursion, and I wouldn't find out about them until they were already in play. I made a mental note to do an audit of her purse before we left.

"Remember," I said, "we're concentrating on blending."

She waved a hand in dismissal. "Why don't you stop wasting time worrying about what I'm going to wear tonight and take a minute to consider what you're wearing now?"

I looked down at the yoga pants and tank top I'd changed into after my shower. "What's wrong with what I have on? This is what I always wear around the house."

And around town, but I didn't figure I needed to expand on my point.

"Exactly," Gertie said. "You haven't ever considered fixing yourself up a little?"

"I have to do that tonight. I see no point in playing dress-up for Carter to come by and bum food off of me."

Gertie sighed. "I am really failing you. You can give the man a sandwich to go, but sometimes dessert first is the best meal."

"You want me to be dessert?" Something about that statement made me more than a little uncomfortable. "Like wear food or something? Is that supposed to be sexy?"

"I don't want you to layer your chest with lunch meat, if that's what you're asking, but a little whipped cream never hurt anyone. You could at least put on a push-up bra. Let the girls peek out of that tank top a bit."

I waved her toward the front door. "I'm not going to show up at the door wearing whipped cream. Sure as shooting if I did that, it would be the UPS man standing there. I will consider the push-up bra if you'll stop giving me dating instructions."

"I will for today except for one last thing," Gertie said as she stepped outside. "Do everything I would do. That gives you plenty of wiggle room."

It gave me room to jog from here to California, but I just nodded and waited until she'd reached the sidewalk before heading into the kitchen to see what kind of leftovers I had for Carter. I gave two seconds of thought, as promised, to the push-up bra, then dismissed it completely and pulled a dish of casserole out of the refrigerator. Carter had already seen plenty of my lean body and completely average chest. A bra wasn't going to fool him.

I was heating up chicken casserole when I heard the screen door open and Carter call out.

"In the kitchen," I said.

He walked in as I pulled the casserole from the microwave. "I love a woman in the kitchen," he said with a smile.

"It's a good thing," I said. "Because I love being in the kitchen. Just not for the cooking part."

"That smells delicious," he said. "Ally or Gertie?"

"Gertie's chicken casserole. I have cookies from Ally. Something new. Chocolate cookies with peanut butter chips."

"Sounds incredible."

"They are. We could probably end wars using them as a negotiating tool."

As I placed the plate of heated casserole on the table, he stepped up next to me and pulled me close to him, lowering his lips to mine. I wrapped my arms around him and pressed my hands into his muscular back. As the kiss deepened, I moved closer, molding our bodies together.

Carter groaned and broke off the kiss. "If you keep touching me like that, I'll end up missing a meal and being late back to the office."

"Might be worth it," I said, completely surprising myself.

I'd been dancing around taking our relationship to the next level for a while. At first, I'd been dead set against a deep physical and emotional commitment because one, I was lying to Carter about who I was, and two, I was planning on returning to my old life as soon as I was able. Now that I had decided to leave the CIA and had Gertie and Ida Belle trying to convince me to relocate to Sinful, what had been a recipe for certain heartbreak before, could be the start of the best thing that had ever happened to me.

I found that concept both exciting and scary as hell.

He stared at me a bit longer, looking almost as surprised at my statement as I felt.

"I have no doubt at all that it would be worth it, and if I had anyone but Quincy and Petey sitting in that jail, I'd call Celia right now and give her my resignation by phone."

He ran one hand through his hair. "God, I can't believe I'm asking this, but can I get a rain check?"

"I don't know. I might be busy later on."

"I'll make sure I'm worth the wait."

He grinned and kissed me hard on the mouth again, then slid into a chair. I pulled a beer out of the refrigerator and ran it across my forehead before pulling out a second and putting them both on the table. I had no doubt he'd be worth the wait. I'd had a hot flash standing in front of an open refrigerator.

"You look exhausted," I said as I took a seat across from him.

"I am. Haven't slept much lately. I was hoping to get the situation with the poacher under control before word got out, but this deal with Petey launched it right out of orbit."

"Ida Belle told me about Petey's past and his issues. It doesn't sound like he could be the poacher."

"He's not, but the state has enough evidence to force me to hold him."

"I know you can't tell me what the evidence is, but could they be mistaken?"

"The evidence exists, if that's what you're asking, and unfortunately, it does point to Petey being the poacher, but there's got to be another explanation."

"Like what?"

He narrowed his eyes at me. "Like a number of things, none of which I can share with you. I need you to trust me when I say I'm spending every waking moment working on this."

"When you're not dealing with Celia, you mean."

"That woman. Don't get me started. I assume you heard about Buddy Riker's dogs getting out?"

Since both Ida Belle and Gertie had been briefly present at the scene of the crochet crime, I nodded. "Gertie said they chased her all the way from the butcher and they ate all her hot links. She was practically in heart attack mode when she ran into the General Store. Walter and I were about ready to call 911. Ida Belle said she was talking to Dorothy and took off when she saw Gertie running."

"Smart woman," Carter said. "If Gertie's running, there's usually a good reason for it."

He proceeded to give me his version of the fray, complete with a pause and grimace over the part about Celia's underwear. Fortunately, the story was just as funny as seeing it in person and the retelling I'd done for Walter, and I laughed the entire time Carter was describing what had happened.

"That's hilarious," I said. "I wish I could have seen it. Minus the underwear part, of course."

"Of course. Anyway, Celia is insisting that you had something to do with it, even though she apparently saw you go into the General Store and Walter verifies that you were right there talking to him when all hell broke loose."

"Why doesn't she believe Walter?" I asked. "It's not like he'd lie for me."

Carter snorted. "Walter is half in love with you. If he were thirty years younger, I'd have some serious competition." He stared at me a moment, then smiled. "I think you remind him of Ida Belle. You know, when she was younger."

"So I'm like the daughter they could have had?"

"God help us all, but yeah, I could see that."

"Well, good thing I'm not, or me and you would be first cousins."

"Gross."

I laughed. "So what happened with the dogs?"

"They took off with the most god-awful scarf I've ever seen, and Deputy Breaux managed to round them up with some hot dogs a couple blocks away."

"Why would dogs want a scarf?"

"I have no idea. Maybe they thought it was a rope. Tiny likes to play tug-of-war. Anyway, the long and short of it is, the dogs knocked Dorothy and Celia down, mangled a sewing bag and a skirt, and stole a scarf. Buddy is insisting the gate was closed and Celia is insisting I arrest the dogs."

"Of course she is. I'm surprised she didn't just order you to shoot them."

"That was her first command. She moved on to arresting when I refused."

Guilt coursed through me. I hadn't thought the dog plan through well enough, and now Celia was trying to give Carter and the dogs the raw end of it.

"I hope the dogs don't get into trouble," I said.

"Do you really think I'd let a couple of hounds having some fun get hauled off to the pound over Celia? You should know better."

"So what did you do?"

He grinned. "I told Celia that if she didn't go home and shut up about it, I'd arrest her for indecent exposure."

"You didn't!"

"Bet on it. I haven't seen someone turn that red since last year's holiday bonfire. By that time, a crowd was starting to form out back, and amidst the pointing and snickering, Celia decided it was a good idea to leave."

I shook my head. "I almost feel like the fate of humanity is riding on the election recount."

"The fate of humanity in Sinful probably is. If Celia remains mayor, I give this place a year before it's a ghost town. Everyone who's not in jail will have moved."

"I guess all the people who voted for her should have put a little more thought into the process."

"Too many Catholics won't vote for a Baptist. A whole other bloc of idiots still think Marie killed her husband, even though we know that's not the case. The general population trends to older around here, and sometimes it's hard to get older people to change their thinking on something once they've made their minds up."

"I bet a lot of them are rethinking things now."

Carter nodded. "I'm sure they are, but it's too late. If the recount stands, Sinful is stuck with her for four years."

I sighed. I didn't want to think about the fallout if Celia remained mayor. I was just now tossing around the idea of becoming a regular around town. If I moved here and the people I cared about left, then I'd be adrift all over again. I frowned, realizing I was feeling nostalgic about a place I'd spent a tiny fraction of my life in. Sometimes it scared me how quickly I'd changed. Had I always been unhappy in my former life and just convinced myself otherwise? Or had coming to Sinful opened my eyes to what my life could be if I didn't follow in my father's footsteps?

"Have you given any more thought to your plans once Ahmad is out of play?" Carter asked.

He watched me closely as he asked the question, and I wondered for a moment if he knew me well enough that he could predict my thoughts or if they'd simply shown on my face. He'd tried to make the question sound casual, but there was an edge to his voice that he couldn't hide. My answer was important to him, but he'd left this question off the table for a while now. I knew he was giving me room to make decisions, but his tone left no doubt that he was heavily invested in my answer.

"It's just about the only thing I have thought about," I said.

"And have you reached any conclusions?"

I shook my head. It was one thing to mull over my prospects with Ida Belle and Gertie, but it was completely another to lay them out for Carter, especially when I didn't feel like anything had been decided. Gertie and Ida Belle cared about me and would miss me if I left, but it wasn't the same. I didn't want to get Carter's hopes up only to change my mind when the time came to, as Gertie would say, fish or cut bait.

"Nothing is set in stone," I said. "I know I can't go back to the CIA. Too many things have happened. I'm not the same person who stepped off the bus that day I arrived here, and I don't think I can ever get that person back."

"Would you want to?"

"No. Don't get me wrong, I'm not ashamed of who I was or anything. My job was important, and I did a lot for this country, even if no one will ever know. I spent every waking hour that I wasn't on assignment training to make myself a better agent. I was loyal, dedicated, and I was damned good at it."

"I don't have any doubt that was the case."

"But...I don't know. It was like, no matter how good I was or how successful the mission, there was always something missing. I can't explain it because I don't really understand it myself."

"I get it. I felt the same way in the Marine Corps. I knew the service I provided was invaluable, and that there were only a handful of people who could have performed at the same level. I was proud of my ability and my accomplishments, but I was never satisfied."

"Yes! That's the word—satisfied. I've been downright ecstatic, but I don't think I've ever been satisfied. Why do you think that is?"

"Because it's not your place." He leaned back in his chair. "You know, I could be a shrimper. I worked on boats when I was a teen, and growing up here, there's not much I don't know about the profession. And I'm sure I'd be good at it. But I don't think I'd ever come home at night and flop down in my recliner and feel satisfied with my day."

"But you do now?"

He nodded. "I know that from where you sit that might be hard to believe, and I'll be the first to admit that lately, it's been harder than it has to be. The politics of the situation are enough to make me want to run screaming in the streets, but I still feel like this is where I belong. I had to go halfway around the world to figure that out, but once I did, I haven't had a moment of doubt."

"Not even one?"

He smiled. "Well, maybe one. Or two. Since you arrived, anyway."

"I really messed up your perfect little world, didn't I?"

He reached across the table and took my hand. "If it was really that perfect, you couldn't have affected it. Getting involved with you hasn't been without some hard moments. I've had to revisit things I never wanted to think about again. But I'm drawn to you like a moon to its orbit. I tried to fight it for a long time. Now I'm just praying I don't get damaged in a cosmic explosion."

"If there's an explosion, it's more likely Gertie did it. But I get what you're saying. I tried to stay away from you, and you see how that worked out."

He grinned and went back to eating. "I'm irresistible."

"Clearly." I slumped back in my chair and sighed. "Sometimes I think I should just chuck it all, live on a boat, and get a job sacking groceries at the General Store. Walter would hire me."

"Maybe you could take up that librarian thing for real."

"It's too quiet in libraries. I'd be bored to death. There's probably rarely any shooting."

"If part of your job criteria is shooting things, then you'd be bored in most professions. Not a lot of shooting goes on in the General Store."

I grinned. "It might if I was working there."

"Ha. Please don't make my job any harder."

"That's what worries me the most. Not making your job harder. I don't have an ounce of guilt over that." I frowned. "I worry that I'll change everything and I still won't be happy."

"That was my biggest concern when I came back here and took the deputy job. I had tried other things and traveled around the world, so I thought I knew what I wanted, but there's always that doubt, you know?"

"Actually, I don't know. This is the first time in my life that it hasn't been laid out in front of me like a map. I never thought about what I wanted to do. Not like I'm doing now. I just did what everyone thought I would do and worked hard to be the best at it. I'm almost embarrassed to admit that it never went beyond that."

"You lost your mother when you were young," Carter said quietly, "and it doesn't sound like your father took much of an interest in your ability to cope. I had my mother and Walter. They kept me straight and focused—as well as anyone can keep a boy focused while he's becoming a man."

"My father never took an interest in anything but his work. I look back now and wonder how he and my mother ever got together. She was exactly the opposite of him."

"Maybe she thought she could fix him. She wouldn't be the first or the last woman to walk down that path."

I nodded and stared down at the table. Every time I thought about my mother I got sad. When I thought about my father, I got angry. Thinking about both sort of canceled the feelings out but left me even more confused about what I should think about all of it.

"So what are you doing tonight?" Carter asked, changing the subject.

"Nothing earth-shattering." I hoped. "Probably just hanging out with Gertie and Ida Belle. Gertie's a little sad over losing Godzilla."

Carter shook his head. "Every time I think I've seen it all that woman invents a new way to surprise me."

"Me too. But at least it's never boring."

I hoped I didn't have to eat those words.

Chapter Thirteen

At eight o'clock that night, I was dressed for what I prayed would be my first uneventful excursion to the Swamp Bar. I didn't have high hopes, mind you, but wishful thinking had gotten me through the evening. That and watching Gertie wave cookies at the water for a solid three hours. Despite her attempts to bring Godzilla out to play, the gator was still in hiding. That bit of fortune had encouraged me to believe I might get lucky twice in one night.

I had on a pair of jeans that looked about ten years old even though I'd pulled the tags off of them that evening, a Metallica T-shirt, and a pair of running shoes. I had dark black liner around my eyes and sparkly blue eye shadow. My lipstick was blood red, and because I wasn't exactly a welcome figure at the Swamp Bar, due to a couple of past situations, I had donned a wig with straight black hair and teased it a bit at the roots, giving me a sort of '80s rocker look. If I didn't blend, I wasn't sure who would.

I exited my room and knocked on Gertie's door. "You ready?"

"I'm in the kitchen," she called back.

I headed downstairs, praying that Gertie had taken my casual dress comment seriously, but part of me was still afraid she was standing in my kitchen dressed like Queen Elizabeth or a sexy nurse. I let out a sigh of relief when I saw her. I wasn't a fan of skinny jeans, but they were so much better than the alternatives that I wasn't about to complain.

Aside from the jeans, she wore a New Orleans Saints T-shirt and tennis shoes. Her hair had been teased into a big poof on top of her head and she'd painted in a big magenta streak, giving her a trendy sort of skunk look. To complete the picture, she had purple eye shadow complemented by way too much blush and lipstick that matched the stripe in her hair. She looked me up and down and nodded.

"The wig is a nice touch. It's boring, but you'll fit right in," she said. "You'd look better with a tattoo."

"No way." The last time Gertie put a temporary tattoo on me, it turned out to be not so temporary.

"Just a little one? I have a cute rose that would look great on your biceps."

"No roses, cute or otherwise. I thought I was going to need a skin graft before I got the last one off."

I heard the front door open and yelled out, "We're back here."

Several seconds later, Ida Belle walked into the kitchen and I nodded in approval. She had old jeans that looked like they'd been rolling around under a car for a while, a *Sons of Anarchy* T-shirt, and a ball cap that said "I'd rather be fishing."

"Nice," Gertie said. "Maybe a tattoo—"

"No tattoos," Ida Belle interrupted.

"You guys are no fun," Gertie complained. "I buy the wrong package one time and you never want to try it again. Well, you can be boring all you like, but I'm sporting my tattoo."

We both looked at her. No tattoo was visible, so if she planned on sporting one it either wasn't on her yet, or was in a place she wasn't currently sporting. Which led to a whole other series of worries.

"Where is your tattoo?" Ida Belle asked, apparently drawing the same conclusion I had.

"That's for me to know and hot guys at the Swamp Bar to find out," Gertie said.

"Guess we're safe then," I said. The only hot guy I'd seen anywhere near the Swamp Bar was Carter, and he'd been there on a professional basis, not as a customer.

"Everyone got their phone charged?" Ida Belle asked.

Gertie and I nodded.

"Let's go over the plan one more time," Ida Belle said. "We split up when we get to the bar and circulate some, listening for any conversation about the poaching or any mentions of Petey and Quincy. If we get an opportunity, we introduce the topic and look for reactions. We get a picture of anyone we think might be the poacher, *making sure* they don't notice."

Ida Belle gave Gertie a hard look as she delivered the last sentence.

"I got it," Gertie said. "Pictures, boring, discreet."

"Then I head out of the bar to check out boats," Ida Belle said, "while you two keep watch to warn me if anyone leaves the bar."

"And if someone sees you on the dock?" Gertie asked.

Ida Belle pulled a package of cigarettes from her back pocket. "I say I stepped out to have a smoke."

I nodded. "Good thinking. Tomorrow morning, we collect all the pictures, isolate faces, and get them in front of Petey."

"How are we going to do that?" Gertie asked. "Walter can't keep carting you into the sheriff's department in a crate. Carter might get suspicious if Walter never delivers some actual product."

"I've got this one," Ida Belle said. "Gertie will attempt to visit Quincy, as she's family. If Carter still can't risk letting her in, then Myrtle will slip Quincy a prepaid cell phone loaded with the pictures."

"Nice," I said, and gave her an approving nod. "Simple and doesn't require anyone to run from dogs."

"Whoot!" Gertie said, and pressed her hands in the air. "Ida Belle will make notes on boats that fit the description Hot Rod gave and we'll figure out who owns them."

"It sounds so organized," I said. "It almost scares me. Is there anything we haven't thought of?"

"Where's Carter tonight?" Gertie asked.

"He's staying at the office until midnight, then Sheriff Lee is going to spell him."

Ida Belle stared. "That old coot Lee hasn't been up past eight o'clock since Eisenhower was in office."

"There's nothing they can do about it," I said. "Deputy Breaux was up all last night sitting with the drunks, and still worked until noon. Carter probably hasn't slept but a handful of hours in the last couple days, and Celia's insisting that there be a law enforcement office present as long as someone is being held in the jail, so Myrtle can't manage it alone."

"The drunks all got out this afternoon," Gertie said. "Petey and Quincy are the only ones there, and they're hardly going to stage a breakout."

"It's Celia being Celia," Ida Belle said. "If Lee's asleep at the wheel, then so be it. At least Celia can't blame Carter. Lee is the sheriff."

"She'd find a way to blame him anyway," Ida Belle said, "but all that's neither here nor there. The thing I was most worried about is covered—Carter won't be dropping by Fortune's house to check in."

"Unless he shows up for a midnight booty call," Gertie said, far too gleefully.

"There will not be any midnight booty calls," I said. "Me and my booty would like to be in bed and asleep before midnight."

Gertie sighed. "You really need to step up your game."

"I'm hardly going to have a booty call with you sleeping across the hall," I said.

"It would be the closest she's come to sex in a century," Ida Belle said.

"How would you know?" Gertie said. "I'll have you know, I've got plenty of men interested in me."

Ida Belle waved a hand in dismissal. "There aren't enough men in Sinful with hearts good enough to be interested in you. They'd be dropping like flies."

"Maybe you'll find a young one at the Swamp Bar using your tattoo," I said.

Gertie perked up. "Ooooohhhh."

Ida Belle looked pained. "I'll remind you, before you encourage her to seek out strange men for one-night stands, that she's currently living in your house."

I cringed. "Good point. Okay, let's get this circus on the road."

I was a little surprised at the amount of restraint Ida Belle showed driving to the bar. Not once did I see the speedometer hit over ninety. Granted, since we were on a one-lane dirt road that wound like a snake and had no shoulder except marsh and bayou, it was still a little much. But we managed to arrive in one piece and my pulse hadn't hit training rate yet. Gertie, with her bad day vision and even worse night vision, probably hadn't even realized how fast we were going.

"Oh," Gertie said as we parked across the parking lot from the dilapidated shack that fronted as a bar. "It's karaoke night." She pointed to a sign on the door.

"Don't even think about it," I said. "We're supposed to maintain a low profile and besides, you and I can't sing worth crap."

"I can sing," Gertie said.

"They won't even let you in the church choir," Ida Belle said, "and that's with taking into account the joyful noise and all."

"I could rap," Gertie said.

"How in the world is a two-thousand-year-old rapping woman wearing leggings and makeup like a party clown supposed to blend?" Ida Belle asked.

"These aren't leggings," Gertie said. "They're skinny jeans."

"The hell they are," Ida Belle said. "They don't make you look one bit skinnier."

"The jeans are skinny," I explained. "Not necessarily the person wearing them."

"Well, it ought not be allowed," Ida Belle said.

"I'll have you know," Gertie said, "I'm three pounds lighter."

"That's because Fortune removed a pipe wrench from your purse before we left the house," Ida Belle said. "That doesn't count."

"It doesn't matter," I said, heading them off before they got too distracted and forgot the objective. "Even if we were all runway models, none of us would sing. Everyone in a bar looking directly at you is the exact opposite of flying under radar."

"Fine," Gertie said. "But next time we have a couple days available, we're going to New Orleans to a karaoke bar."

"Whatever," I said, figuring it was a safe enough bet. Given the way things had gone since I'd been in Sinful, the likelihood of having a couple days available was slim, especially since I'd just had a couple of blissful peace. I figured I'd used up all my karmic peaceful markers.

And even if we ended up with time to take the trip, at least no one would be depending on our performance to get them out of jail. Ida Belle and I could sit in a corner and drink until we were deaf.

"Leave your purse," Ida Belle said to Gertie.

Gertie shook her head. "No way. I have important stuff in here."

"You have stuff that will get you into trouble in there," I said. "And as much as I hate to admit it, we usually don't get to walk out of here and that thing weighs at least fifteen pounds. Leave it. It will either get you caught or identified."

"Fine," Gertie said and put her purse on the floorboard.

We climbed out of the SUV and headed to the bar. At the bottom of the steps leading up to the porch, Ida Belle motioned to me. "You go in first. I figure you should sit at the counter. That's where all the young, single, hot women always are in the movies."

"Then I should sit at the bar as well," Gertie said.

"Based on that criteria," Ida Belle said, "you should be sitting back at your house. Just go in a minute after Fortune and work the left side of the room. I'll take the right."

I headed up the steps, took a deep breath, and opened the door to the bar. Country music blared so loud it made me wince, but at least it was the jukebox. I said a quick prayer that they turned the volume down before drunken amateurs started singing and headed straight back for the counter, trying to avoid eye contact with anyone on my way.

I'd learned the hard way that eye contact in a bar was a dangerous thing, especially a place like the Swamp Bar. If you looked too long at a woman, she thought you had a problem with her and wanted to fight. If you looked too long at a man, he thought you wanted to have sex. Which often led back around to a woman wanting to fight, especially if she'd already set her sights on the man. I'd never considered myself hot, but by Swamp Bar standards, I was practically a runway model.

There was an empty stool at one end of the bar and I slid onto it. The bartender gave me the once-over, then nodded. Apparently, I'd passed inspection. I recognized him from my previous trips and knew he was one of the brothers that owned the bar. I just wasn't sure if he was Whiskey or Nickel. Whiskey being for the brother's preference in drink, and Nickel referring to a five-year stint in prison.

"Whaddayawant?" he asked, the entire sentence coming out as one word.

It didn't rank high on the customer service scale, but at least he hadn't recognized me. "Beer," I said. "Whatever's on tap."

He nodded and poured a mug, then shoved it in front of me. "One dollar."

"Seriously?"

"It's dollar beer night for all the hotties. Stick around till closing and I'll show you what else you can get for free."

It would have been better if I could have smiled, but the best I could manage was avoiding a grimace. I took a sip of the beer. "We'll see."

He winked and headed to the other side of the bar to break up an arm-wrestling match that had already taken out four peoples' drinks. I turned around and looked across the bar, finally spotting Ida Belle and Gertie. Ida Belle was sitting on a windowsill at the back of the bar, in a perfect position to hear conversation at the two tables in front of her, just as soon as someone turned the music down. Once the karaoke got started, there would be time in between the singing.

Gertie was standing near a dartboard, watching some men play a round and reading some sort of card. I glanced back at the bar where I'd seen a similar card and groaned. It was the karaoke list. If she started singing, Ida Belle might just leave her here to fend for herself. And that was the best-case scenario. I'd heard Gertie sing. Worst case, if she sang too early and everyone wasn't drunk yet, the whole bar would leave.

Behind me, I heard the word "gator" and leaned back on my stool, trying to listen in on the conversation. With the music still blaring, I couldn't catch anything but snatches of sentences, but I picked up "special cut," "ridiculous price," and "making a name." Then they grabbed another round of beer and headed off for the dartboard. I pulled out my phone and sent Gertie a text to get a pic of them and try to listen in if they were talking while playing.

I worried that she might not hear her phone and hoped she'd put it on vibrate. A second later, she pulled it out of the front of her T-shirt. I supposed that made sense. Given that the floor was shaking from the loud music and because it was probably about to cave in, you might not even notice a vibration in your pocket. But on your boobs was a different story. I turned back to the bar and started scanning the people sitting around it, trying to zero in on my next target. As I was inspecting a couple of burly-looking guys at the far corner, the bartender stepped directly in front of me, blocking my view.

"You hungry?" he asked.

"Not if you're on the menu," I said.

He grinned. "A like a woman with a smart mouth. But I was talking about real food. We've got barbecue gator tonight with Cajun fries. On special for $15.99 a plate. That's a three-dollar discount just for you, sweetheart."

I frowned. I was no gator expert, but I knew Francine

charged way less than that when she served it at the café. "That's a little steep, isn't it?" I asked. "Does it come with gold plating or something?"

"Nah, nothing like that. It's just a special cut. Way better than average gator. You know, like them high-end steak places have better cuts than the grocery store."

I had no idea if he was pulling my leg or not, but at those prices, I didn't think the gator would exactly be flying out the door. Not with a crowd more concerned with spending their money on cigarettes and booze. But then I supposed if they were drunk enough and hungry, they might go for it. Which meant Whiskey was either the smartest businessman I'd met or the dumbest. I already knew which way I was leaning.

"I guess it's hard to get this time of year," I said. "That would affect price, too."

"It can be hard, but I stocked up earlier this year. Now I gotta make room for the new season coming up."

"It sounds good," I said. "Do you do the barbecue yourself?"

"Why? You like a man who can cook?"

"It doesn't hurt."

He nodded. "I do all the barbecue and the smoked meats. I'll be serving it in about ten minutes. Let me know if you're interested. Word got around that I was cooking up something special, so it's gonna go fast. But I'll make sure you get some if you want it."

He winked and headed through the door at the back of the bar that I presumed led into the kitchen. My phone buzzed and I looked down. It was a text from Ida Belle.

You getting anything from that moron?

I tapped in my response.

Yeah. Hit on. If he does it again, I'm going to shoot him. Also, he's serving BBQ gator tonight at really high prices.

Her reply was instant.

Really? Get a pic.

I sighed. I knew it had to be done, but the last thing I wanted was that idiot thinking I was interested in him. And he would definitely take it that way. The kitchen door opened and he stepped back behind the bar. I motioned him over.

"I think I'd like to try that gator," I said.

"Great. You wanna try anything else?"

"I'm still thinking about the anything else. I'm one of those old-fashioned sort of girls. But I wondered if I could get a picture with you? You know…something to help me with my thinking after tonight."

He looked disappointed when he realized that he wasn't getting lucky tonight but not completely defeated since he thought the picture meant he was still in the game.

"I'll just lean across the counter," I said and put my phone out in front of me.

He leaned in and put his arm around me. I'm sure it was completely by accident—not!—that his hand just happened to rest over my breast. I took the picture and even though I was momentarily blinded by the flash, I managed to spin out from under his arm so fast, I thought I'd given myself whiplash.

He laughed. "Name's Whiskey, by the way," he said as he headed back to the kitchen.

I turned around on the stool and saw Ida Belle shaking her head.

I lifted my phone and sent her a text.

Not the first bad guy who's grabbed my boob.

A few seconds later, I got her response.

Probably not the last either.

I rubbed my eyes and created a text to both Gertie and Ida

Belle, more concerned about a bigger problem than random boob assaults.

It's too dark in here. You can't get a picture without flash.

Seconds later, I got a reply from Ida Belle.

So hit on anyone you think is a good candidate and get a selfie with them.

Gertie chimed in.

That's a great idea. I have my eye on a live one playing darts.

Good God.

I grabbed my beer and slid off the stool, somewhat depressed. Was this what I had to look forward to as a detective? A career of random boob-grabbing from bad guys? If so, I was investing in padded bras. It probably wouldn't hurt in the looks department if I was trying for that kind of attention, and at least there would be more man-made items between dudes' hands and my naturally occurring items.

I was just about to move to the far side of the bar and see if I could get anything from the two men at the end when the door opened and a familiar face walked in. I whirled around and sent Ida Belle a text.

That game warden that almost ran into us just walked into the bar.

Chapter Fourteen

I turned slightly on my stool, trying to see where he'd gone, then almost had a heart attack when he stepped up beside me. I dropped my head down and opened Facebook, pretending I was engrossed in the feed. As I leaned farther over the counter and tilted my head a bit to the right, a hunk of black hair dropped across my shoulders and onto my chest. I was ready to grab it and fling it off of me when I remember I was wearing a wig, which meant the lock I'd been ready to fling was attached to it.

It also meant the game warden wouldn't recognize me.

Whiskey walked back out of the kitchen and looked my direction. The grin he'd been wearing disappeared completely as he locked eyes on the game warden. He approached us without even looking at me.

"Help you?" Whiskey asked.

"Jack and Coke," the game warden said.

Whiskey tossed a few ice cubes in a glass, poured in some Jack Daniel's and dashed it off with soda, then he pushed it across the bar. "Eight dollars."

The game warden stared at him for a couple of seconds, the tension between the two of them so high I could almost see it. Finally, he pulled out his wallet and tossed a ten-dollar bill on the counter. "Keep the change."

Whiskey scowled as the game warden slid off his stool and headed toward the two men I'd been about to check out. I repositioned myself on the stool. They would have to wait. The last thing I needed was the game warden thinking I was stalking him. I already had one too many on the hook and hadn't even been in the bar fifteen minutes.

"Friend of yours?" I asked.

Whiskey snorted. "Not hardly."

"You own the place, right?"

"Yeah. Me and my brother."

"Then tell him to leave. If I owned a joint and someone I didn't like came inside, I'd invite them to walk right back out."

He frowned. "Normally, I would, although 'invite' is too nice a word for what I'd do, but in this case, I ain't go no choice. He's Joe Law."

I glanced over at the game warden again, feigning disbelief. "He's a cop?"

"Worse. Game warden. Runs around in a boat all day busting hungry people for catching too many fish."

"Oh. Someone told me the other day that game wardens can just walk in and poke around in your house—dig in your underwear drawer and everything—and without even having a warrant."

"That's true enough. They're supposed to have reason to suspect someone is committing a crime, but that hasn't stopped them from harassing folks who weren't doing anything."

"I can't imagine he'd be popular with the crowd here," I said. "Why do you think he's here?"

Whiskey shook his head. "I don't know, but I don't like it. A lot of other people in here won't like it either." He headed back into the kitchen.

I couldn't say I was exactly thrilled to see the game warden there, but I did find it interesting. The Swamp Bar wasn't the sort of place reputable people hung out. So why was he there?

Especially since he claimed he had his man with Petey. Did he have questions about the evidence as we did? Had he heard about the special barbecue gator being served at the bar and decided to check it out himself?

I watched as the game warden talked with the two men at the end of the bar. Neither of them looked pleased to be interrupted. He wasn't there very long before he turned and headed back in my direction. I started to flee, not wanting to risk being recognized, but then decided to stay put. He'd taken a hard look at me before. If he hadn't recognized me then, he shouldn't now.

He slid onto the stool next to me and gave me a once-over. "You from around here?"

I struggled to keep from rolling my eyes at such a clichéd opening.

"Atlanta," I said. "Got a cousin in New Orleans I came to visit. She talked about this place so I figured I'd check it out before I headed home."

"Your cousin likes this place?"

"No. She hates it. Said it was a wart on the butt of humanity and was single-handedly lowering the IQ of the state. Hell, I couldn't resist."

He laughed. "Bit of a goody two-shoes, your cousin?"

"Just a bit," I said. "You live around here?"

"Couple towns over. What's your name?"

"Susie."

"Nice to meet you, Susie. My name's Trevor."

"You come here for the barbecue or to get your IQ lowered?"

He let out a single laugh. "Definitely the barbecue. A friend told me I shouldn't miss it when Whiskey cooks again. I wasn't in town last time he offered it."

"So it's good, huh?"

"Supposed to be the best."

"Price seems a little high, but I said I'd have a plate. So are you a shrimper?"

He looked somewhat insulted. "No. I'm a game warden."

"Really? That sounds like an interesting job. You catch any criminals this week?"

"Got a poacher sitting in jail in Sinful."

"What was he poaching?"

"Alligators."

I shook my head, attempting to look impressed. "Isn't that something. You don't hear about that kind of thing in Atlanta. This poacher, is he dangerous? I mean, other than to alligators?"

He frowned. "Doesn't appear to be. Seems a little slow if you ask me, but he was caught red-handed. You never can tell about some people."

"I bet you're really smart. How did you catch him? Did you set a trap or was it some of that fancy CSI stuff I see on TV?" I chugged back a huge gulp of beer after delivering that piece of nonsense, afraid I might choke on the words.

"Nothing so elaborate. Just following up on an anonymous tip. A lot of cases are solved that way."

"Anonymous tip. Well, thank Jesus there's always a good citizen around."

"Not always. I do plenty of my own fieldwork."

I struggled not to roll my eyes. "I'm sure you do."

"Yeah, I'm wrapping things up here. Got an offer from the state of Florida so I'll be headed out in a couple weeks."

"That's great," I said, keeping my response brief.

I figured I had exhausted what little information I was going to get out of him and needed to get away before he took things in a personal direction. He'd already spent more time staring at my chest than my face, so I had a good idea where the conversation would veer off and I wasn't interested in pretending any longer.

"If you'll excuse me," I said. "Little girls' room."

I jumped off the stool and headed for the hallway at the back of the bar with a sign that read "Crappers" above the entry. You had to give the place points for keeping it classy. I wondered if they actually had toilets inside and not just a hole in the floor.

The bathroom looked like it was on a quarterly cleaning schedule, but there was soap and running water and two stalls that contained actual toilets. I didn't have to go, thank God, because if ever there was a reason to hold it, I was looking at it. I took a minute to check my wig in the cracked mirror and wiped a bit of smeared mascara out from under one of my eyes. I reached for paper towel to wipe it off and had a thought.

A padded bra would have to wait for a trip to New Orleans, but I could pad my own right here. At least then the next guy who tried to feel me up during a selfie would only be grabbing cheap paper towels. I pulled a couple sheets of the towel off the roll and folded it into a square, then stuffed it in my bra. I turned from side to side, checking out the difference, then repeated the process and stuffed a second layer. It wouldn't amount to much of a visual difference in the dim light of the bar, but the layers of padding definitely reduced the ick factor of potential groping, which reduced the potential of my breaking someone's hand before I remembered the mission.

I fixed up the other side to match the first, then headed out of the restroom, scanning the room for the game warden as I stepped into the mix of people. I didn't see him where I'd left him at the bar, so I pulled out my phone and sent Ida Belle a text.

Where is game warden?

Her reply came a couple seconds later.

Near dartboards.

A moment of worry zipped through me but then I remembered the game warden hadn't seen Gertie that day. Only Ida Belle and me.

Another text from Ida Belle came through.

I'm heading outside to check out boats. Let me know when someone is leaving the bar.

I texted a response, then made my way through a crowd of people dancing and scanned the counter. I hoped I could engage the two men I'd had on radar before now that the game warden was out of the way. I headed to the far end of the bar, happy to see that they were still on the same stools and a stool next to them was being vacated by an old man who looked as though he wasn't going to live long enough to make it out the front door.

I slipped onto the stool and nodded at the two men as I sat.

First guy. Six feet even. One ninety-five. Good muscle tone. No visible flaws other than the fact that he's in the Swamp Bar.

Second guy. Six feet two. Two sixty-five. Looks like he stepped out of an offensive line and into the bar.

I wasn't overly worried about either one of them as a single threat, but put together, in a crowded bar, they made a fairly lethal combination. They both checked me out, then apparently finding me an acceptable interruption, one of them launched into conversation.

"You the broad with the game warden?" he asked.

"God no!" I said. "I'm not a big fan of most law enforcement. Spend a lot of time harassing regular folk while getting paid by our tax dollars. Can't help who hits on me at a bar, though, can I?"

They both grinned and I figured I'd passed the test.

"I'm Buck," the first guy said. "This is Trick."

"Trick?" I asked.

"Momma was expecting a girl," Trick said. "Said she was tricked."

"If your birth size was comparable to your adult size," I said, "I can see why she felt that way."

They laughed.

"I think I was a pretty big one," Trick said. "She talks about it every year on my birthday—thirty-two hours of labor, all that crap."

"Given that it probably took the Jaws of Life to deliver you," I said, "you ought to be giving your momma gifts on your birthday." I looked across the room toward the dartboard and saw the game warden watching the players.

"I saw that warden guy over here earlier," I said. "Was he hassling you about something?"

They both frowned, and I wondered if I'd changed tracks too soon.

"We're shrimpers," Buck said. "He started asking us about dead alligators and bait lines. We don't know nothing about that."

I noticed that he seemed to rush that last statement in and dropped his gaze from mine in favor of looking at his glass of whiskey.

Trick nodded. "Alligators ain't our thing. I mean, I like to eat 'em just like the next guy, but I ain't about hunting 'em, especially out of season."

"He told me he'd caught the guy," I said.

"Really?" Buck asked. "Sure didn't seem that way with all his questions."

"If someone got popped for it, Hazard would know," Trick said.

Before I could even wonder about the name "Hazard," Buck put his fingers in his mouth and whistled. I covered my ears with my hands, but it was already too late. Might as well have had a locomotive blowing its horn right next to me. The train horn must have gotten Hazard's attention as well because Buck started waving one hand, gesturing for someone to come over.

A couple seconds later, the tallest, biggest guy I'd seen since I arrived in Sinful stepped up next to us and I understood the name. This guy was the bull in the china closet.

Six feet seven. Three hundred eighty pounds. Winded from walking maybe fifteen feet. Threat level nil. Could get away from him with a slow crawl.

"What's up?" Hazard asked.

"That nosy game warden is in the bar. Told this woman that he caught the poacher. You hear anything about that?"

Hazard scowled. "Yeah, I heard all right. They got that screwed-up kid in jail."

"What screwed-up kid?" Trick asked.

"The one that ain't right in the head," Hazard said. "His buddy got eaten by that gator years back."

Trick's eyes widened. "You talking about Petey?"

"Yeah, that's him," Hazard said.

"What the hell?" Buck asked. "That's the dumbest thing I ever heard."

Hazard shrugged. "Maybe. The kid's big though. I mean, if he wanted to, he could kill a gator and haul it in a boat."

"I guess so," Trick said, "but I don't see it."

"The kid wouldn't be in jail if they didn't have something on him, right?" I asked. "I mean, unless the local cops are that dumb or that corrupt."

Trick frowned. "Sheriff Lee's old as dirt and probably hasn't thought longer than two minutes running since before I was born, but I went to school with Carter. He's a deputy but he's the one handling things. He ain't stupid."

"No," Buck agreed. "And there ain't no love lost between me and cops but I never heard anything about Carter being corrupt. Would surprise me if I did."

Trick nodded. "Former military, town hero type."

"So why's he got the kid in jail?" I asked.

"That's a damned good question," Trick said. "I think I might just go over there and ask our friend the game warden. I got a cousin that ain't right. It's dirty dog shit to mess with someone like that."

Before I could formulate an argument for staying put, Trick jumped off his stool and started toward the dartboard, a determined look on his face. If I had to place bets, the game warden was going to come out the big physical loser in this one, and Trick would be keeping Quincy and Petey company when it was all said and done.

"Oh man," Buck said, and headed after Trick.

Hazard shrugged and lumbered off in the direction he'd come from, apparently not interested in the short-lived fight that was probably coming. I slipped off my stool and started toward the dartboard, staying far enough away to avoid the fray but making sure I could text Ida Belle if things got out of hand. The last thing I needed was a fight moving outside while she was poking around on peoples' boats.

"Hey." Trick grabbed Trevor's shoulder and pulled him around.

At that exact moment, the music ended and the general conversations in the bar trickled off as people pointed to the two men. I looked over at Gertie, who was standing in the dartboard area, the table with darts on one side and the dance floor on the other. She glanced over at me and I gave her a single shake of my head. This was one of those times where blending was definitely the best option.

Trevor started to puff up until he realized he was staring directly at Trick's chest. He took a step backward. "Can I help you?" he said.

I gave him points for managing to keep his voice normal, but anyone with even a little training could see he was unnerved. He'd already glanced around, checking his options for a quick exit.

"Yeah," Trick said. "You can tell me why you got Petey locked up for poaching."

Trevor's eyes widened a little and I could tell he'd figured out that nothing he said was going to appease the angry man in front of him.

"I can't talk about an open investigation," Trevor said.

"It ain't open if you got a boy sitting in jail."

"It's open until it goes to trial."

"Trial? Are you kidding me? Is the state going to explain how a boy who doesn't even go in the water managed to poach alligators? What kind of trumped-up crap are you running here?"

The noise level in the bar ticked up slightly as people began whispering. Trevor licked his lips and glanced again toward the exit door. Blocking his sprint to safety was about thirty people, several clustered around the dartboard, waiting to see if Trick decided to take his conversation with Trevor to the next level.

"Look," Trevor said. "I got an anonymous tip and found evidence in the boy's boat and on his person. The state said it was enough to lock him up and issued the order. I don't make that decision."

"Of course you don't. You're just a pissant game warden, running around the bayou and picking on traumatized kids. Nice job you've got. You and the state need an ass-whupping."

Whiskey walked out from behind the bar and toward the two men. "Break it up," he said. "I don't want any trouble in here. A bunch of people were hauled out last night. One of these days, all this fighting is going to get us shut down."

"Get this rat out of your bar," Trick said, "and there won't be any fighting."

Trick looked over at Whiskey. "He put Petey Hebert in jail for poaching."

Whiskey's eyes widened and he looked back and forth between Trevor and Trick, like he was waiting for the punch line.

"You're serious?" Whiskey finally asked. "I don't believe it."

"Ask him," Trick said. "Or call up Carter. You'd believe him, right?"

Whiskey blew out a breath and shook his head. "Mister," he said to Trevor, "I think you've opened a can of worms that you didn't expect. It might be best if you clear out."

Trevor looked at Whiskey. "You sure about that?"

Everyone else probably didn't notice Whiskey's hesitation. It was only a fraction of a second, but I saw the tiny twitch in his jaw before he answered. "I'm sure."

"Fine," Trevor said. "I'll leave."

He delivered those words with a bit of an edge, trying to keep up the tough guy persona, but I could tell he was relieved to have a reason to leave and a clear path out of the bar.

As Trevor started for the door, a man playing darts stepped up to Whiskey. "Hey, man, I forgot to tell you but I saw someone poking around your boat when I got here—about an hour ago."

I frowned. Ida Belle hadn't been out there that long, so this man must have seen someone else.

Whiskey glanced at Trevor's retreating figure, narrowing his eyes, then back at the man. "You're sure it was my boat?"

"Looked like it. Evinrude motor with a red racing stripe?"

"Yeah, that's mine."

Oh no. I pulled out my phone and sent Ida Belle a text.

Clear the area now!

"Looks like someone's out there now," someone yelled from the back of the bar. "Can't see crap through these windows."

"What the hell?" Whiskey set off for the door and I gave Gertie a panicked look. Ida Belle wouldn't have time to vacate if we didn't slow Whiskey down. Unfortunately, I had been standing behind him, so short of tackling him from the back, which would probably look suspicious, I didn't have a way of stopping him.

Gertie must have understood the necessity of keeping Whiskey from racing out the door because she launched into action. Just not the action I would have chosen. I was thinking maybe tripping and falling in front of him or into him. Even ten seconds more would give Ida Belle the time she needed to clear out from the pier and get to her truck.

But Gertie never did things the easy way.

She grabbed a handful of darts from the table nearby and tossed one at Whiskey. Except that it didn't hit Whiskey. It sailed right over his head and landed square in the middle of my left boob. People around me sucked in a breath as I yanked the dart out while simultaneously giving thanks for the paper towel padding, but before I could say anything, Gertie had fired again. This time, the dart hit Whiskey in the forehead.

He stopped dead in his tracks and yelled so loudly, I swear the floor shook. Then he yanked the dart from his head and shook it at Gertie. "You crazy old bitch."

Gertie took one more shot at him, this time the dart landing in his leg, and then she took off running. People moved to the side, clearing a path out the front door, probably figuring they were better off with the crazy outside, especially as she was still clutching two more darts. Whiskey brushed the dart from his leg and set out after her, the stunned patrons staring in silence. I hurried behind them, trying not to draw attention to myself. As I exited the bar, I saw a group of men walking toward me from the parking lot.

"Grab that woman!" Whiskey shouted.

Chapter Fifteen

Gertie veered left and sprinted for the pier, moving faster than I thought possible. Whiskey jumped off the porch and ran after her. I hurried down the steps, scanning the pier and parking lot for Ida Belle, but didn't see her. Bar patrons began to stream out of the bar and onto the porch, some of them now hurrying to the pier behind Whiskey.

I'd lost sight of Gertie and Whiskey as soon as they got out of the porch light because there were no lights past that. A tiny fleck of light bounced up and down in the distance, and I figured it must be Gertie using her cell phone as a flashlight. I hurried to the pier with the rest of the patrons, pulling my nine-millimeter from my waist, and hoping that I really didn't have to shoot Whiskey before the night was over.

When I got to the dock, I heard the roar of a boat engine, and Whiskey started yelling. "She's stealing my boat! That crazy old woman is in my boat!"

The clouds parted enough to allow a stream of moonlight through and I watched as Whiskey's boat streaked away from the pier and down the bayou.

"I've got a boat here," Buck yelled. "Let's go after her."

For the first time ever, while on a mission, I froze. Clearly, I couldn't shoot them, but if they caught up with Gertie, what would they do to her? Maybe I could shoot the boat, but then they'd turn on me, and there were a lot more boats, so shooting one didn't fix anything.

I felt a tug on my arm and turned around to find Ida Belle standing behind me. "Let's get out of here," she whispered, and hurried through the crowd now gathered at the pier.

I cast one last glance down the bayou but Gertie and the boat had disappeared into darkness. I heard another boat engine fire up as I rushed out of the crowd behind Ida Belle. Her SUV was parked at the back of the lot, far enough away from the crowd that no one said anything as she started up her hopped-up engine and headed away from the bar. She waited until we'd gone a scary fifty yards or so before turning on the headlights and punching her foot down on the accelerator.

"We can't leave Gertie out there," I said, clutching the grab bar as the SUV took a huge bounce in an enormous pothole.

"Don't have a choice. We can't steal a boat, and as awesome as this truck is, it still doesn't float. Don't worry. Gertie knows these bayous better than anyone. She'll head back to town and ditch the boat. We just need to get to Sinful and watch for her."

I had no doubt that Gertie knew the bayous around Sinful as well as the next resident, but I also knew she couldn't see for crap during the day, much less running in moonlight in a stranger's boat that she wasn't used to handling. Ida Belle had sounded convincing when she'd delivered her opinion, but I saw her clenched jaw and her iron grip on the steering wheel and knew she was worried.

"What happened?" she asked.

I started filling her in on the showdown in the bar and had just told her about the dart when I saw something move in the marsh on our left. "What is that?" I asked, leaning over the center console toward the driver's-side window, trying to make out the fast-moving object.

As Ida Belle rolled down the window to get a better look,

the object took a hard right and came straight at us. Ida Belle slammed on the brakes as the boat flew up the embankment and slid across the road. The SUV wheels locked up, sliding on the dirt road, and rolled right over the boat as if it were a speed bump.

Before it even came to a complete stop, I jumped out of the SUV and ran behind it, praying that Gertie had been thrown clear of the boat before the SUV had flattened it. A rush of relief came over me when I saw the totaled but empty boat sitting in the middle of the road. As Ida Belle rushed up beside me, I heard a groan coming from the weeds.

We ran over to the edge of the road and found Gertie crawling out of the marsh. She was covered in mud and had marsh grass clinging to her but appeared to be okay. A boat engine roared nearby and Ida Belle and I grabbed Gertie's shoulders at the same time and hauled her up, then half dragged her to the SUV.

Ida Belle threw open the back and we tossed Gertie inside before she could even get a word out. We hurried back inside the vehicle and Ida Belle tore off down the road as if we were being chased by a tornado, and that wasn't far from the truth.

"Are you all right?" I called back to Gertie.

She groaned again, and her head peeked up over the backseat. "I have a headache."

"You're lucky you're not dead," Ida Belle said. "What kind of move was that?"

"The boat was running out of gas," Gertie said. "I saw the SUV and figured my only chance to get away was to catch a ride."

"That's a hell of a way to go about hitchhiking," I said.

The SUV hit another hole and Gertie flew up, almost hitting her head on the roof of the vehicle.

185

"Do you have to hit every hole on the road?" she complained.

"Only if you want me to keep driving," Ida Belle said.

"It's painful riding back here," Gertie said. "Slow down so I can crawl into the backseat."

"If you get into my backseat with all that mud and grass on you," Ida Belle said, "you'll be cleaning this truck for the next ten years."

"At least throw me a rag or something," Gertie said. "I've got mud and swamp water in my eyes."

I looked over at Ida Belle, who shook her head. "I didn't think to stock that kind of stuff."

"What about in your purse?" I asked Gertie.

"I took the towel out to make room for the pipe wrench," Gertie said.

I was about to attempt to tear off some of my T-shirt when I remembered the paper towels. I reached into my bra and pulled out a wad of the paper and tossed it back to Gertie.

"Incoming!" I yelled.

Ida Belle glanced over at me, one eyebrow raised.

"I improvised until I can get a padded bra," I said.

"Ah," Ida Belle said. "The gropers."

I scanned the road in front of us, looking for a landmark that would tell me how much farther we had to go to reach the highway, but I still hadn't learned to read tree stumps and cattails.

"How far are we from the highway?" I asked. I wasn't worried about Whiskey and Buck catching us, and no one from the Swamp Bar was going to come remotely close in a vehicle either, but I'd bet money someone had called the cops. We needed to hit the highway before Carter or Deputy Breaux got onto this road.

Ida Belle must have read my mind because she yelled at us to hold on and slammed her foot on the accelerator. The SUV launched forward, then banged through another hole so fast I swear it was airborne for a couple of seconds. I braced my feet on the floorboard and managed to get my seat belt on before we flew in and out of the next dip. I heard Gertie banging around in the back and hoped she was still in one piece when we got back to Sinful.

"Is anyone following us?" Ida Belle asked.

I turned around and looked out the back window. "I don't see any headlights. Even if Whiskey found his boat and called for someone to come get him, it would take time for them to get to him. And no way would they catch us, not in anything I saw in the parking lot. I'm more worried about Carter or Deputy Breaux getting here before we get out."

Ida Belle nodded and her shoulders relaxed a tiny bit, but she didn't slow down at all. We slid and bounced for another five minutes or so before sliding onto the highway. Ida Belle didn't even pause before flooring it and we raced for Sinful at light speed, never passing another car. About a half mile from town, she slowed to the speed limit and we drove onto Main Street, looking between buildings at the bayou, but everything appeared quiet.

"I bet no one is available to go to the bar right now," I said. "With someone having to sit at the jail twenty-four-seven and working the poacher case, they're limited on people."

"And a ruckus at the Swamp Bar would be low on the list of priorities," Ida Belle said.

"I need a tranquilizer," Gertie said. "My entire body hurts."

"I have some horse tranquilizers," Ida Belle said. "Keep up that whining and I'm going to grant your wish."

I wasn't about to ask why Ida Belle had horse tranquilizers, because there might come a time when they came in handy. I just hoped she had them hidden well enough that Gertie couldn't find them.

When we pulled up in Ida Belle's garage and the door closed behind us, I let out a huge breath of relief. We helped Gertie out of the back of the SUV and Ida Belle pointed to the door that led to the backyard.

"Outside," Ida Belle said. "You have to hose down before you're allowed in my house."

Gertie mumbled something about prison treatment but walked out back and stood behind the patio while Ida Belle sprayed off the thick layer of mud and grass. When she was finally satisfied, Ida Belle turned off the hose and headed up the steps to the house.

"I'll turn off the porch light," Ida Belle said. "Lose the clothes. I'll toss you a towel and you can head straight for the shower."

"You want me to undress out here?" Gertie asked.

"*Now* she's worried about being discreet," Ida Belle said as she walked inside.

The porch light went off and a couple seconds later a towel flew out of the door and landed on Gertie's head. Deciding I didn't want to get any more personal with Gertie than I already was, I hurried inside and left her to the disrobing. Ida Belle handed me a shot glass as soon as I stepped inside.

"I have wine," she said, "but no way was that going to do."

I tossed back the shot and felt my throat start to burn. "What is this?"

"Our new brew of cough syrup."

My vision blurred for a moment. "Is the goal to prevent coughing by knocking people out?"

"Something like that."

"Then you're good. Give me another."

Ida Belle poured us each another shot and we finished them up as Gertie stalked inside, glaring at Ida Belle as she headed down the hall for the bathroom.

"You got any aspirin?" I asked.

She grabbed a bottle from a cabinet and tossed it to me. "Headache?" she asked.

"Yeah, I think I hit the top of the SUV a couple times on the way home."

"I better take some to Gertie, then," Ida Belle said. "If you've got a headache, she must be working up a migraine."

She left the kitchen, and I tossed back the aspirin and downed it with a third shot of whiskey. It made my eyes water, but almost immediately, my head started to feel better. Or maybe I just couldn't feel my head. Either way, it worked.

Ida Belle came back into the kitchen and grabbed a dishrag. She wet it and rubbed it across her eyes, removing the dark makeup.

"You got another one of those?" I asked. "My eyes feel like they're glued in place."

She wet another towel and tossed it to me. I climbed onto a barstool and started wiping the goo off my face. "How do women do this every day?" I asked. "It's like someone dumped dirt in my eyes."

"I never did like makeup," Ida Belle said. "Makes my skin itch, but it's a good thing we looked the way we did tonight. Hopefully, no one recognized Gertie. Otherwise we're in a heap of trouble."

"No one said anything," I said. "Even the people who know her wouldn't expect her to be in the Swamp Bar. And the lighting is really bad in there."

Ida Belle nodded. "Let's just hope it was dark enough. And

that no one—"

Ida Belle frowned and pulled her cell phone out of her pocket.

"It's from Myrtle," she said. "Carter's looking for us."

"Crap." That was never a good sign.

Ida Belle flew into action. She threw open the pantry and pulled out a bag of microwave popcorn, tossed it in the microwave, and fired it up. Then she grabbed a packet of cheddar cheese garnish for the popcorn, opened it and started flinging it around the kitchen.

I stared at her, certain she'd gone mad.

She tossed the packet on the cabinet and whirled around. "Turn on the TV and the DVD player. Start the DVD, then hit Pause."

I must have hesitated for too long because she yelled, "Move!"

If there was one thing I understood and knew how to respond to, it was taking an order. I had no idea what Ida Belle had up her sleeve, but clearly she was working off a master plan. I ran into the living room and set up the TV as Ida Belle instructed. I heard her down the hall talking to Gertie, but I couldn't make out what she was saying.

She rushed through the kitchen a couple seconds later and out the back door. I stood there staring as she ran back inside and into the laundry room with Gertie's dirty clothes.

"Grab the popcorn out of the microwave and pour it in a bowl," she called out as she ran by.

I located a large plastic bowl in the cabinets and poured the popcorn into it. I'd just put it on the counter when I heard a knock at the front door. Ida Belle hurried out of the laundry room.

"Get the door," she said. "It's movie night."

I spun around and took a single step for the front door when I felt my head being tugged from behind.

"The wig," Ida Belle said as she yanked it off my head.

I'm pretty sure a good hunk of my own hair went with it, but I pulled what was left into a ponytail and knotted it on the back of my neck. I kicked off my tennis shoes in front of the couch and opened the door.

Chapter Sixteen

Carter stood on the porch and he stared at me, looking a bit taken aback. "You're here."

"It appears so. Did you need Ida Belle?"

"Sort of."

"Well, then you should sort of come inside. She's in the kitchen."

Carter stepped inside and followed me back to the kitchen where Ida Belle was scrubbing the cheddar cheese off the cabinets. I figured the best thing I could do was keep my mouth shut and let Ida Belle work her plan.

"What are you guys up to?" he asked.

"Movie night," Ida Belle said.

"She's making us watch the Fast and Furious movies again," I said, referencing the DVD I had queued up in the living room.

"Gertie's here, too?" he asked.

"In the shower," Ida Belle said. She waved a hand at the scattered cheddar cheese. "She had a run-in with the popcorn garnish."

He reached over and brushed some off my shoulder. "I see."

"Who's there?" I heard Gertie shouting from the bathroom.

"It's Carter!" Ida Belle shouted. "You better not be dripping on my hardwood floors."

We heard the bathroom door slam shut, and Ida Belle

shook her head. "You want something to drink?" Ida Belle asked.

Carter shook his head. "No. I've got to get back to the sheriff's department."

Ida Belle stopped cleaning and looked at him. "Any particular reason you stopped by?"

"I got a call from Whiskey at the Swamp Bar," Carter said. "He said an old woman assaulted him with darts and stole a boat."

"And you immediately thought of us," Ida Belle said. "How charming."

Carter shuffled a bit. "Well, I, uh, thought I'd work this one from an elimination standpoint."

Ida Belle narrowed her eyes at him. "You going to knock on the door of every senior citizen in Sinful, are you?"

Carter opened his mouth, then closed it again.

"Didn't think so," Ida Belle said. "Well, now that you've done a bed check, can the prisoners get back to their free time?"

"Sure," Carter said, and looked over at me. "I'll call you tomorrow."

"Great," I said, enjoying his discomfort entirely too much.

I walked him to the door, gave him a good-night kiss, then headed back into the kitchen. "Oh my God," I said. "You are a genius. You came up with all of that in minutes. And he bought it."

Ida Belle nodded. "Because it was decidedly typical of Gertie but not so absurd it made him suspicious. And as much as I would like to take credit for lightning-fast critical thinking, I had all afternoon to plan."

"You planned this before we went to the bar? Why?"

She let out a single laugh. "You have to ask?"

"Never mind. I need to take lessons from you. I never get

things by Carter that easily."

"That's because you're always winging it, but you'll improve."

I grinned. "I suppose you have had a century to practice covering up for Gertie."

"Not quite a century," she said drily, "but long enough."

"Is it safe to come out?" Gertie's voice sounded behind me and I turned around to find her standing there wearing a fluffy blue bathrobe and a towel wrapped around her head.

Ida Belle shook her head. "It's a little late to ask now, but yes."

"You told her to stay in the bathroom?" I asked. The one worry I'd had when the whole thing was going down was that Gertie would come out of the bathroom and totally blow Ida Belle's performance.

"I told her to stay in the bathroom but yell out the door asking who it was," Ida Belle said. "I was afraid Carter wouldn't believe we were all here if he didn't at least hear her voice."

"Perfect," I said. The voice ensured he knew she was in the house, but being holed up in the bathroom ensured Gertie couldn't poke a hole in Ida Belle's carefully crafted plan.

Ida Belle plopped the bowl of popcorn on the bar and pulled three beers out of the refrigerator. "Let's go over what we found out. Then we'll get some real food going. Fortune?"

I told them about my conversations with Whiskey, Buck, Trick, and Trevor, careful to explain my perceptions of the men as I went.

"So," I said when I was done, "it's clear that Whiskey was uncomfortable with Trevor being in the bar, and he's serving up alligator off-season, claiming it's some kind of special cut. Is there such thing?"

Ida Belle shook her head. "There's alligator tail and alligator tail. He's probably spouting that other nonsense so he can sell at a premium."

"Wouldn't locals know the difference?" I asked.

"Who knows?" Ida Belle said. "Some of them will believe anything, especially if Whiskey feeds them a line of bull after they've been drinking a while."

"What about Buck?" I asked. "He seemed a little edgy talking about poaching. It was so slight a regular person wouldn't have noticed, but it was definitely there."

"He's clever," Gertie said. "And sly. Always gave teachers fits. You wouldn't think it to look and talk to him, but rest assured, something's always processing in that mind of his."

"So he's capable?" I asked.

Gertie nodded. "Very capable, I'd say."

"Okay," I said. "I know my next question isn't going to be popular, but we have to cover everything. Is there any chance that Trevor is right about Petey? Even that giant guy, Hazard, suggested Petey was strong enough to do it, and I assume he'd have the knowledge."

Gertie and Ida Belle both frowned, and they were silent for a long time. Finally, Ida Belle said, "Neither one of us wants to think it, but you're right to bring it up. We wouldn't be very good detectives if we didn't consider all the possibilities."

"So?" I asked. "What do you think?"

"I think he's got the strength," Gertie said, "and he probably hates alligators enough to want them dead, but I still can't get past the water part of things."

"Ramona saw him getting closer every time she spotted him," I reminded them.

Ida Belle shook her head. "Anything is possible, but standing on the bank is still a huge gap from driving a boat around, especially at night. I can't imagine Petey could sneak out without Quincy noticing."

"He couldn't," Gertie said. "He put a security system on the house before he brought Petey home from the hospital. The doctors warned him that Petey was already trying to wander."

"Okay," I said. A good deal of the poaching was probably done at night, so it added another layer of difficulty to Petey's ability to pull it off. I wasn't crossing him off the list altogether, but he was at the very bottom.

"What about the boats?" I asked Ida Belle.

"I found several with Evinrude motors, but didn't get to search through them all before Gertie started a fray. I got pictures of several that I want to check out."

Gertie started bouncing up and down on her stool like a six-year-old. "I found something in the boat I stole. When I hit the bank, the top of the cooler popped open and an alligator skin flew out and hit me smack in the face. I tried to find it, but it fell off when I hit the water."

I stared at her. "And you're just telling us this now?"

Gertie put her hands on her hips. "I was a little preoccupied on the ride home, trying to keep from dying in that death-mobile. Then Ida Belle put me through her new prisoner processing routine, then Carter showed up. And what difference does it make anyway? Were you going to stick around and look for it? Stick around and hope Carter showed up before Whiskey so you could turn over the evidence?"

"I guess not," I said, "but you don't have to be so grumpy about it."

"You didn't have to ride in the back without a seat belt or a seat," Gertie said.

"I also didn't throw a dart in your boob," I said.

"Oh yeah," Gertie mumbled. "Never mind."

"You're sure it was gator skin?" Ida Belle asked, getting us back on task.

"Positive," Gertie said, "and based on the smell, it was fairly fresh."

"That was Whiskey's boat," Ida Belle said.

I frowned. "Was it?"

"He said it was when he took out after Gertie," Ida Belle said.

I nodded. "Yes, but a guy in the bar told him someone was in his boat so that's the assumption he made when he went outside, but Carter said Whiskey called him to report *a* boat being stolen, not *his* boat."

"You think that means something?" Gertie asked.

"Maybe. Maybe not," I said. "Were there two boats at the pier that looked similar enough that he could confuse them in the dark?"

"Yeah," Ida Belle said. "As a matter of fact, the boat right next to his was the same model and had the same engine."

"Red stripe on the motor?" I asked.

She nodded. "But I don't have any idea who the second boat belonged to."

"I think I might," I said. "Buck is the one who took Whiskey to chase Gertie. They were headed for the same place Whiskey's boat was docked when I made my exit."

"But you're not sure they got in the matching boat," Ida Belle said.

I shook my head. "And I only got a picture of Whiskey. I don't have one of Buck. We need to figure out whose boat Gertie stole. That skin seals it."

"Do you think we could get it out of Carter?" Gertie asked.

"I don't know," I said. "I mean, it's not the sort of thing we'd normally have a conversation about."

"Meaning, he'd be suspicious right away," Ida Belle said. "I suppose we could always check tomorrow and see if the boat is at the Swamp Bar. If it's there, then the stolen boat wasn't Whiskey's and could be Buck's."

"What if he's not at the bar during the day?" I asked. "Just because the boat's not there doesn't automatically make the stolen one Whiskey's. He could be out fishing or have it somewhere else. Do you know where Whiskey lives?"

"At the bar," Ida Belle said. "There's a couple rooms off the kitchen. Whiskey and Nickel live there. Their dad lives in his old house off the highway to New Orleans."

"So if we check out the bar, we might run into both brothers and in daylight," I said. "That's not good."

"I don't think so," Ida Belle said. "I wondered why I didn't see Nickel last night and asked someone at the bar. They said he was in jail in New Orleans and wouldn't be out for a week or so."

"Okay, so only Whiskey is in residence right now," I said. "And if the boat's there, we push him down on the suspect list. What about Buck?"

Ida Belle shook her head. "He lives in an apartment somewhere up the highway. I don't know where he keeps his fishing boat."

"He wouldn't keep it with his shrimp boat?" I asked.

"No," Ida Belle said. "They pay a premium for large slips down at the shrimp house. He's probably got his fishing boat somewhere else."

"Like maybe the place where Petey's boat was?" I asked as a thought occurred to me. "Do either of you know what kind of engine is on Petey's boat?"

Gertie's eyes widened. "It's an Evinrude. I remember when Quincy bought it."

Ida Belle whistled. "Whoever set Petey up made sure they

did a good job of it, down to picking the same engine. If the state found out about Hot Rod, he could be called to testify, and that engine is the only thing he'd be able to give them."

I nodded. "And if they asked other people if they'd noticed anything suspicious, they might also point to the same engine. I have to give the poacher credit. It's the perfect plan."

"Clever," Gertie said. "Which points more to Buck than Whiskey."

"So tomorrow, we find out whose boat is missing," I said. "Then we decide what to do with that information."

"Sounds like a plan," Ida Belle said. "Now, let's get some steaks on the grill. I'm starving."

———

I spent a good portion of the night nursing the headache, which had returned full force as soon as the whiskey wore off. Since Gertie had already taken control of my one and only ice pack, I'd sat on the couch for hours with a bag of frozen strawberries on top of my head, waiting for the headache to subside. Finally, I'd thawed out the strawberries, so I put them in the sink and headed up to bed around 4:00 a.m. I'd threatened Gertie with bodily harm if she woke me up for anything other than a house fire or the death of someone relevant, and was hoping to get some sleep now that my head had stopped pounding.

I was awakened by my cell phone.

I opened one eye and saw light streaming into the room at the edges of the blinds. It was morning, but it sure didn't feel as if I'd been in bed for long. I lifted my phone and groaned. Carter was calling me at 7:00 a.m. That was never a good thing.

I answered the phone, waiting for the inevitable yelling about car chases and boat stealing, but he went a whole other direction.

"Have you seen Gertie this morning?" he asked.

Since I'd seen her after midnight, I'd technically seen her this morning, but I figured this wasn't the time for exactness.

"No," I said. "I was still asleep. Is something wrong?"

"I've gotten five frantic phone calls in the last ten minutes. Every one of them claiming she's walking an alligator down the street on a leash. Please tell me that's not possible. That the people in this town are experiencing a joint hallucination. That it's an illegal drug experiment being conducted by our government. Anything."

I jumped out of bed and walked across the hall to the guest room. Gertie's bed was empty and her nightgown was neatly folded on the end of the bed.

"I don't know what to tell you," I said. "She spent the night here, but her room's empty and the bed is made."

"You told me you were putting that alligator back in the swamp."

"We did. I swear."

"Uh-huh. And what swamp did you put him in?"

"The one behind my house."

"Jesus H. Christ. It didn't occur to you that would be a problem?"

"Of course not. Why would it occur to me that a wild animal given a choice of freedom or walking around like a dog on a lead would chose a collar and hanging out with Gertie on pavement? Where did you expect us to take him? Florida?"

"Farther away would have been nice. Anyway, I've got the state on the way to my office in ten minutes. Sheriff Lee isn't answering the phone—probably asleep at his desk—and Deputy Breaux is trying to sort out the mess that went down at the Swamp Bar last night. I need you to handle the situation with

Gertie or I'm sending the state over to deal with her and that gator when they get here."

"What do you want me to do?"

"Get them off the sidewalk and put that animal back in the water."

Chapter Seventeen

Carter disconnected the call, and I tossed the phone on my bed and pulled on some clothes. As I was walking downstairs, I dialed Ida Belle, who took forever to answer and sounded half asleep.

"We've got trouble," I said.

"Can it wait another hour?"

"Not according to Carter." I filled her in on Gertie and Godzilla's latest adventure.

"We've got to get them off the sidewalk and Godzilla back in the water," I said.

"Until the poacher is caught, she's not going to leave that alligator alone."

"Well, what are we supposed to do about it? We can't lock it up somewhere, and she's managed to tame the darn thing. It can't hang out behind my house. It's likely to walk into anyone's backyard and demand baked goods."

"Let me get dressed and head over there. Maybe I'll think of something on the way."

"I've already thought of something. Barbecue. I'm going outside to look for them. I'll text you if I find them."

I disconnected the call and headed outside to locate Gertie. The people who'd complained all lived north of me toward the park, so I set out that way at a medium-paced jog. It didn't take me long to figure out where Gertie was. All I had to do was follow the screaming.

I picked up pace, rounded the corner, and spotted the problem right away. A woman, a man, and two boys, probably five and two, were standing on top of a car parked at the curb and looking down at Godzilla, who was wearing a pink collar and staring up at them hissing. As I got closer, I realized the youngest boy was clutching a small package of chocolate chip cookies.

At the end of the street, I saw Gertie round the corner in what I assumed was supposed to be a jog, but it looked more like a limp. I watched as she got slower and slower and finally slowed to barely a walk. At the rate she was going, the car would rust out from under those people before she showed up and collected the gator.

I moved to the sidewalk and crept slowly toward the vehicle. When I was about twenty feet away, I stopped and waved, trying to get their attention, but it did no good. Their backs were to me and they were all fixated on Godzilla. Not that I blamed them. Sure, people from Sinful saw alligators all the time, but they usually weren't accosted by them in the middle of the street, and I was guessing that they'd never seen one sporting a collar.

"Hey," I said, hoping my voice projected enough for them to hear but not so loud that it got Godzilla's attention.

No one showed any sign of moving, so I tried again, this time a little louder. The wife turned slightly, frowning, and when she caught sight of me, her eyes widened and she started shaking her head and waving her hands.

"Run! Get help!"

I waved my hand in a downward fashion, trying to get her to lower her voice, but she was stressed and it was too late. A couple seconds later, Godzilla walked around the side of the car and stared right at me. He hissed and pushed up on his legs. This was so not good. I had my gun this time, but I couldn't take a shot at him in the middle of the street. Not with the risk of a ricochet.

My second of hesitation was all he needed to launch. I whipped my head around, looking for the nearest tree, but all I saw was small ornamental trees and bushes. I could probably outrun him onto a porch, but I'd already seen him climb stairs, so unless I burst through someone's front door, that wasn't going to work either.

Godzilla launched, racing toward me and surprising me all over again with his speed. The woman started screaming, and the kids began crying. I crouched, only one option left, and waited until the gator was about five feet away, then I sprinted straight toward him and jumped. The gator threw his head up and I heard his powerful jaws snap together as I cleared his tail. As soon as my feet hit the ground, I took three giant bounds, then leaped onto the hood of the car and ran up on the top to stand with the others.

"You're Superwoman," the oldest kid said.

"Something like that," I said, and watched as Godzilla whipped around and ran back to the car, settling in where he'd been before.

I leaned over to look at the youngest kid. "Can I have those cookies?"

The mother's eyes widened. "You ran up here to take a toddler's cookies? What kind of crazy are you?"

"They're not for me," I said. "The gator likes cookies. That's probably why he cornered you. He saw the package."

Clearly, she didn't buy it. "I'm calling the police again. This is ridiculous."

"The police are who sent me," I said. "Believe it if you want or don't, but that alligator is not going to move away from this car until he gets those cookies. And I can outrun him. If you want to sit here all day, I'm happy to go back home and have breakfast."

The woman, who was clearly to the point of hysteria, grabbed my arm and pushed me. "Get off. I don't care if he eats you. You're some sort of psycho."

Lucky for me, she was weak and I had awesome balance, because the shove barely moved me, but it did piss me off. Her husband was panicking, his hands on her arms, trying to get her to let me go. The kids were wailing again and I'd had about all I could stand of everything.

I came around with my right hand and slapped the woman in the face. She jerked back, shocked, and let go of my arm. Before she could react, I grabbed the cookies out of the toddler's hand and sprang off the car, waving the package at Godzilla. He shifted his body around and started out after me. I ran down the block toward Gertie, slowing only long enough to toss a cookie onto the pavement. I was down to my last one when I reached the end of the block where Gertie had finally gotten up and was standing with the broken leash.

"You're on your own," I yelled.

I tossed the last cookie onto the ground in front of her, then veered off to the left and jumped into the bed of a passing pickup truck. The truck driver slammed on the brakes and leaned out of his window, staring at the alligator as Gertie tied the leash around the pink collar.

"Are you crazy?" he yelled at Gertie.

It seemed to be the question of the day. Unfortunately, I was leaning toward a big "yes" in response.

"I'm fine," Gertie said. "Just go on about your business."

The driver looked back at me. "Can I drop you off somewhere or are you crazy too?"

I looked down at Gertie and Godzilla, who was now resting quietly beside her, and sighed. "Crazy," I mumbled, and climbed out of the bed of his truck.

He shook his head and tore off down the street, probably afraid whatever was wrong with us was catching. Godzilla took one look at me and hissed, and Gertie tapped him on his head.

"Behave, now," she said. "Fortune gave you cookies. She's your friend."

"I am not his friend. What I am is in the doghouse with Carter, who sent me to get both of you off the sidewalk and that gator back in the water."

"I'm not letting him go back where I found him," Gertie said. "The poacher will get him. At this point, he could catch him with an Oreo or two."

"And whose fault is that?"

"Fine, it's my fault. But he's domesticated now so it's too late."

"Domesticated" was a big leap in describing Godzilla's current state of mind. I could work with opportunist, but I wasn't about to forget that the gator could easily become an apex predator.

"Then put him somewhere else," I said, "but not in my backyard. At this point, the poacher is not your only problem. Carter will shoot that gator in a second to avoid the liability."

"How is Carter liable for something a wild animal does?"

"He wouldn't be, except you made a spectacle of yourself and the gator and people called the police. Now that he's aware of the problem, if he chooses to do nothing about it, then he's liable for anything that happens from this point on."

Gertie's face fell, and I knew it was finally settling in just how easily Celia could use this against Carter if Godzilla bit anyone.

"Fine," she said. "We can turn him loose in the bayou at the back of the subdivision."

I didn't like it. It was way too close to people for my comfort, but I also lacked the equipment to haul him anywhere else. "Fine, but get him there fast," I said.

Gertie headed off down the street, the gator trotting beside her. I hung back a little, not wanting to be any closer to Godzilla than I had to be. It was the most ridiculous sight I'd ever seen. So ridiculous, in fact, that I pulled out my phone and snapped a picture.

Gertie had just stepped into a vacant lot at the end of the block when Ida Belle rounded the corner in her SUV and pulled up beside me.

"Doesn't look like a big emergency to me," Ida Belle said. "At least not on the Gertie scale."

"You should have been here ten minutes ago."

Ida Belle looked behind me. "There's a family standing on top of their car."

"Ten minutes ago," I repeated.

"Ah. So what's she's doing now?"

"Putting Godzilla in the bayou at the end of the subdivision. She refuses to take him farther away from town and honestly, I'm not looking to transport him again, either."

Ida Belle shook her head. "Mark my words, this is not going to end well."

"You don't have to convince me. I stole a toddler's cookies and made him cry. I slapped that hysterical woman on top of the car, who is probably on the phone with Carter right now trying to get me arrested."

"Well, get in, cookie snatcher. The least I can do is buy you breakfast before we head out into the bayou to get into more trouble."

I climbed into the SUV and we watched the clearing. Finally, Gertie stepped out of the trees and headed our way. She climbed into the SUV without a word and let out a long sigh.

"Stop fretting over that gator," Ida Belle said. "All this is going to be over as soon as we figure out who that boat belongs to."

That seemed to perk her up a bit. "Are we going now?"

"After breakfast," Ida Belle said. "Your antics got Fortune and I out of the house without coffee again. I swear I'm going to give you a curfew, but instead of giving you a time that you have to be home, it will be a time you have to wait until you leave the house."

We had breakfast at Francine's, then headed back to Ida Belle's for her to pick up supplies, and she was being very cryptic about exactly what those supplies included. She came out of her garage with a plastic case about two feet square and eight inches high. I'd seen about every weapon known to man and couldn't come up with a single one that fit in a case with those dimensions. I worried a bit about it but not nearly as much as I would have if it had been Gertie toting around a secret weapon.

I insisted on inspecting Gertie's handbag before we started out, and after removing a Taser, two of the four pistols she had, and an entire honey-baked ham, I had the purse weight down to a manageable fifteen pounds or so and the weapons equivalent to that of small country. I checked my full-sized nine and my mini in my foot holster and we headed out to the airboat.

"Are you just going to drive right up to the pier and look at his boat?" I asked as we took our seats.

"I have a plan," Ida Belle said. "Trust me."

Famous last words. I yanked three life jackets out of the storage bench and handed one to Gertie.

"I'm not wearing a vest," Ida Belle said.

"Calm down, Michael Phelps," I said. "The extra is for Gertie to sit on."

I pointed to the bottom of the boat in front of the bench and Gertie groaned.

"Why don't I get to ride in the seat?" she complained.

"Because I only have one ice pack and you commandeered it," I said. "And if you sit on the bench, we run a high risk of having to fish you out of the water. Trust me, you're safer in the bottom."

Gertie grumbled some more but put the life jacket in front of the bench and sank down on it. If we were going to keep using my boat for potentially dangerous ventures, I was going to have to look into putting a legitimate seat down there for Gertie. Either that or side rails on the bench. Maybe a racing harness.

We set out for the Swamp Bar, and I couldn't help feeling odd about approaching the place in daylight. I'd always preferred the cover of dark for missions, but after last night's boat-thieving adventures, my guess was Whiskey would have someone watching the pier at night now. Probably his father, who usually served as a bouncer of sorts. He might not be able to manhandle most of the crowd in the bar, but I had no doubt he could pick off boat thieves with a gun and never even have to stand up to do it. He could just sit there and wait, like using a deer lick.

Besides, we didn't want to wait until night to look into this. I couldn't say why, exactly, but I knew that things were about to reach a head. We needed to zero in on the truth now, because I had a feeling it would either explode in the town's face or slip away before we could pin it down. Neither was a good option, especially with Petey's future on the line.

I knew Ida Belle said she had a plan, but the closer we got to where I thought the Swamp Bar was located, the more antsy I got. It was a marsh. Yes, there was high grass and clumps of trees, but given that the bar was on pylons, someone could see a good distance across the area surrounding the bar if they were standing on the front porch or looking out a window. Added to that, the airboat wasn't exactly stealthy when it came to sound, and noise carried across the marsh something fierce.

We rounded a corner in the channel we were traversing and I spotted the bar in the distance, rising up out of the grass. We were probably within hearing distance, especially if someone was outside. I was just about to force Ida Belle's plan out of her when she cut the engine on the boat. She hopped out of her seat and grabbed an oar from the side of the boat, motioning to me to grab the other.

"We're going with the tide," she said, "so it should be easy to get us farther up. That clump of trees at the bend will hide us from anyone at the bar, even if they're looking from a window."

We started rowing until we reached the trees, which put us about fifty yards away from the bar. Close enough to get a good look at things with binoculars, but not so close that we couldn't get away. If this was Ida Belle's big plan, I approved, but I didn't see the reason for all the secrecy.

Ida Belle put the oar back in the holder and reached down to open the mystery case she'd brought on board. "Now for the fun part."

I leaned over to look inside the case as she opened it, expecting her to pull out some military-grade binoculars, then smiled when I saw the contents. "A drone. So much better than binoculars."

"I assume you've used them before?" Ida Belle asked. "Just probably much better than what I could get off the Internet."

"A couple times," I said, "but my missions usually depend on complete invisibility. A drone flying around sort of gives you away and I'm tasked with getting close enough to get information or kill, so it defeats the purpose."

Ida Belle nodded. "Well, in this case, I figure we only need to get close enough with it to see if the boat is there, and we can fly it over the bar so it can't be seen from inside. Worst case, Whiskey sees it and starts shooting, but from this vantage point, we'd be long gone before he could get to his boat and attempt a chase."

"His boat wouldn't stand a chance against the airboat, anyway," Gertie said. "I can't believe you got one of these. I've been thinking of ordering one. I'm dying to try it out."

"No way," Ida Belle said. "I'm flying the drone. If I have a heart attack or otherwise lose the use of my hands, then Fortune takes over."

"I never get to do anything fun," Gertie said.

"You assaulted a man with darts last night, then stole a boat," I pointed out. "This morning, you scared people so badly they're probably listing their house with a real estate agent as we speak, and all because you thought it would be a good idea to walk an alligator like a dog. Now you're going to tell me that you don't get to have any fun?"

"Okay, maybe a little," Gertie said. "But all of those things were stuff you would have told me not to do if you'd known ahead of time."

"And they all turned out so well," Ida Belle said drily. "You're making our point."

"Fine," Gertie said. "Go on and play with your toys."

Ida Belle pulled the drone out and handed it to me, then accessed the flight app on her phone. "Hold it flat in your palm, above your head," she instructed. "I can launch it from there."

I positioned the drone as she requested and a couple seconds later, the propellers started to spin, eventually reaching enough speed to lift the drone from my hand. Ida Belle sent it up and off to the right, approaching the bar from the back, which had the fewest windows.

We all leaned over to see the camera feed on her phone as she directed the drone to the bar. When the drone got close enough to the bar for the camera to capture a good amount of space, she turned it slightly to the left in order to scan the pier.

"Only one boat there," Gertie said, "and it looks like Whiskey's."

"Is that him walking in the parking lot near the pier?" Ida Belle asked.

I squinted at the phone and shook my head. From the camera's viewpoint, I couldn't see his face but the cadence didn't look right. "I don't think so," I said. "This guy lumbers when he walks. Whiskey has a slow stride but smooth."

The guy looked up enough for us to see his face, and Gertie gasped. "It's Buck."

Chapter Eighteen

"Crap," Ida Belle said. "How are we supposed to know who the boat belongs to when both of them are at the bar?"

"Any cars in the parking lot?" I asked.

Ida Belle shifted the camera to the right so that it captured the parking lot. "Several," she said, "but that doesn't surprise me. A lot of people hitch rides out of there after getting too drunk to drive and pick up their cars the next day. I don't know what kind of vehicle Buck or Whiskey drives so we're at a dead end until someone leaves."

"Hey, do you guys find the timing of this odd?" I asked. "I mean, I didn't see Whiskey chatting with Buck and Trick, so I didn't get the impression they were friends. Just patrons. So why is Buck paying Whiskey a visit in the middle of the day?"

"Good question," Ida Belle said. "If it was Whiskey's boat that was stolen, then it wouldn't make a difference to Buck. If it was Buck's boat that was stolen, he already knows Whiskey doesn't know anything because Buck was the one who helped chase Gertie."

"Exactly," I said. "I think I need to hear their conversation."

"And how do you propose to do that?" Gertie asked. "The drone doesn't have audio and even if it did, you can't just drop it down close enough to pick up sound."

I took a giant leap out of the boat and onto the bank. "I'm

going to get close enough to listen."

"Guys," Ida Belle said. "We have a bigger problem."

"What?" I asked.

"I lost my connection to the drone."

We all looked up and watched as the drone veered to the right, then dropped, coming to rest in a tree.

"Crap," Ida Belle said. "We've got to get it out. If I get close enough to reconnect, I can probably get it dislodged. It's just resting on the top branches."

"At least the camera is still going," Gertie said. "And I can still see Buck. He's knocking on the door but it doesn't look like anyone is answering."

"Whiskey might not be there," I said, "and if he's gone in his vehicle, we still don't know if the boat is his or Buck's. Not unless Buck leaves in it."

"I wish we would have gotten here five minutes earlier," Gertie said. "We would have seen Buck arrive."

"We can still watch him leave," Ida Belle pointed out as she tossed me a rope. "It just might take a while."

I pulled the boat close to the bank and tied it off to a tree branch. Gertie and Ida Belle jumped onto the bank and I scanned the marsh, then motioned to them.

"Follow me," I said. "And watch for my signal to stop. Stay low. No talking once we get going." I looked at Gertie. "And no shooting anything."

"I only have two guns on me," Gertie said. "Can't do much damage with only two."

"You can do enough," I said. "Our goal is to listen to any conversation that happens, recover the drone, and get the hell out before anyone notices we're here."

I turned around and headed into the marsh, picking my way through the brush. We were coming up to the bar from the rear, which meant Buck couldn't see us at all but if Whiskey was in his private quarters in the back, he'd be able to spot us if we didn't crouch a bit to fall below the top of the marsh grass. When we got closer, it would be even riskier as the brush often thinned out, allowing you to see different colors and movement easier.

As we drew closer, Ida Belle grabbed my arm and pointed to the video feed. Buck had walked down the steps, probably to leave, when the door to the bar opened and Whiskey stepped outside. He didn't look happy to see Buck.

"Hurry," I whispered, and took off running for the back of the bar. With both Whiskey and Buck in front, we had a clear path, but I needed to get there fast to hear what they were saying.

When I reached the rear of the bar, I glanced back and saw Ida Belle and Gertie some distance behind me, but I didn't have time to wait on them. I slipped around the side of the bar that was perched on land and inched up to the corner.

I could hear the voices even before I stopped.

"What the hell do you expect me to do about your boat?" Whiskey said. "I didn't steal it. That crazy old broad did. Hell, I thought it was my boat at first, and so did you until we got to the pier."

So the boat belonged to Buck. He was our poacher.

"This ain't about the boat," Buck said. "This is about you setting me up."

"What the hell are you talking about?"

"I saw that alligator hide in the brush on the road next to my boat, and I pulled another piece out of the boat while you were calling the sheriff. I tossed them both as far as I could in the bayou. I bet you were disappointed when Deputy Breaux didn't find them in my boat."

I drew in a breath. Buck wasn't the poacher?

I heard Ida Belle and Gertie come up behind me and I

turned around. They both nodded, letting me know they'd heard Buck's accusation.

"You found gator hides in your boat?" Whiskey asked.

"Don't stand there acting like you didn't know. Selling alligator at the bar when there ain't none to be found for a decent price. The game warden hanging around. You're the poacher. You tried to pin it on that boy, but when you realized that wasn't going to work, you figured you'd pin it on me because our boats look similar."

"I'm not the poacher!" Whiskey yelled. "And I didn't put any hides in your boat because I don't have any hides *to* put in your boat. I damn sure didn't set up that kid. But I'm pretty sure I know who did."

"What do you mean?"

"The guy who did it wasn't trying to set you up. He was trying to set me up and he got the wrong boat."

I remembered the guy in the bar saying he'd seen someone in Whiskey's boat earlier that night. If Whiskey and Buck were both telling the truth, it made sense.

"I don't believe you," Buck said.

Ida Belle jabbed me in the ribs and pointed to the phone. I looked at the video and saw Buck had pulled out a pistol and had it trained on Whiskey.

"You're not going to send me up the river," Buck said.

Whiskey put his hands in the air. "I swear, it wasn't me, man."

"Then who was it?" Buck asked.

"You wouldn't believe me if I told you, but I was going to see Carter today and tell him everything I knew. I swear. I already called him and said I needed to talk."

"You think Carter's gonna take your word for anything?" Buck asked. "You've been drinking too much of your own stock."

"I can prove it," Whiskey said. "He was supposed to go away and I was just going to keep quiet, but when I heard about Petey, I decided I had to tell, even if I go down with him."

"What kind of proof do you have?" Buck asked.

"I don't want to say."

"Seems a strange position to take given that I'm pointing a gun at you," Buck said.

"Can you get a shot?" Ida Belle whispered.

I shook my head. "Based on what? Unless Buck shoots, I don't have grounds."

She got it, but I could tell she didn't like the option any more than I did.

"Tell me what your proof is," Buck said, "or I put one in your knee and go to Carter with *my* proof."

"I swear, I'll go right now," Whiskey said. "You can go with me. Or meet me at the sheriff's department if you don't trust riding with me."

"Okay," Buck said. "I'll follow you, but don't get any funny ideas about losing me."

"I don't think that trip will be necessary, gentlemen."

I knew that voice.

I grabbed Ida Belle's hand and looked down at the video as Trevor stepped out of the marsh, his pistol pointed at Buck. I slowly let out the breath I'd been holding. Trevor *had* been suspicious. That's why he'd been at the bar. Now Trevor could handle things legally and I wouldn't have to shoot anyone. Whiskey could sort out his evidence with the state and Buck could get back to shrimping.

"Put that gun down," Trevor said.

Whiskey and Buck both stared at him, their eyes wide.

"About time you people arrest the right guy," Buck said.

Trevor laughed and Buck stared at him.

"You idiot," Whiskey said. "He's not here to arrest me. He's the poacher."

I froze and stared at the video. Surely I'd heard wrong, but the look on Whiskey's face told me everything I needed to know. I'd completely missed the boat on this one. I'd been collecting evidence against one of the victims, not the perpetrator. And unless I did something, I had no doubt there would be two victims, both in body bags, before this was over.

"I said put the gun down," Trevor repeated.

Buck cursed and tried to spin around to get a shot at Trevor, but Trevor fired before Buck had barely rotated and the shrimper screamed and fell to the ground, clutching his stomach.

"Shoot him," Ida Belle mouthed.

I peered around the corner, but Whiskey was completely blocking my line of fire. I couldn't shoot Trevor without going through Whiskey. I looked at Ida Belle and shook my head, pointing to Whiskey on the video. I pointed to the back of the bar and made a square with my fingers, hoping she'd get that I was going to get inside the bar through an open window. From the front of the bar, I'd have a clean shot. Ida Belle nodded, handed the cell phone to Gertie, and pulled out her pistol, indicating she would cover me from the side.

I hurried to the back of the bar and jumped up, grabbing the windowsill and pulling myself over. I went headfirst through the opening and rolled onto the bedroom floor, taking a half second to be grateful no furniture had been placed there because the rest of the room was cluttered with stuff from the floor almost to the ceiling. I was up in a flash and started winding my way through the bar, trying not to make any noise. One loud creak of a floorboard and Trevor would know someone was inside.

When I walked through the kitchen and out the door behind the counter, I could see Trevor standing there, his pistol leveled at Whiskey, but I was partially blocked by the beams holding up the porch. I needed to get closer. I had to make one kill shot or Trevor would have time to fire at Whiskey. I could hear their voices as I inched across the bar.

"We're going to go inside," Trevor said, "and you're going to give me that proof you claim you have."

"I was lying," Whiskey said. "I don't have anything. I just wanted to get rid of Buck."

"You offered to take him to see the deputy," Trevor said. "If you don't have proof, that's a hell of a bluff, and I just don't buy you being that smart. So turn around and head inside."

I edged up to the window and peered outside. Whiskey had turned around and was slowly walking toward the bar, but now he was blocking me from this angle and I didn't think Ida Belle could make a shot without coming out from the side of the building, completely exposing herself. I hoped she didn't take the chance.

I scanned the other windows in the bar, trying to figure out which one would give me a clear shot without having to traverse the open doorway, when I heard a whirring sound outside. I peered out again just in time to see the drone launch out of the tree and straight at Trevor.

"What the hell?" Trevor yelled as he whirled around, but it was too late.

The drone caught him right in the side of his face and arm, causing him to drop the pistol and stagger back a step. Whiskey, who had turned around when he heard the noise, lunged for Buck's pistol, which was lying on the ground only a couple feet away. Trevor jumped forward and scooped up his gun and I put my pistol in the window, ready to take the shot. Finger on the trigger, I aimed and started to squeeze.

And then a shot rang out. Trevor's eyes widened and a hole appeared in the middle of his shirt. He stared at Whiskey in disbelief, and for good reason. Whiskey had just grabbed Buck's gun but hadn't lifted it yet. I ducked as low as possible but was still able to scan the area. No way Ida Belle had made that shot. It came from the other side of the bar.

Who the hell was out there shooting now? How many poachers were there?

"You can come out now!" Carter's voice boomed from outside.

I stood up and looked out the window as he walked up from the direction of the bayou. He leaned over and took a look at Trevor before moving over to extend a hand to Whiskey. The bar owner hesitated for a bit, clearly in shock, but finally took Carter's hand and allowed himself to be half pulled to a standing position.

"I said you can come out now," Carter repeated. "I know you're here. I saw the airboat behind that clump of trees."

Ida Belle and Gertie came around the corner. Gertie was still clutching the cell phone, but Ida Belle had put her pistol back into hiding. I slipped my nine into my waistband and headed out the front door. The gig was up. At least this time we hadn't killed anyone.

Whiskey looked back and forth from Ida Belle and Gertie to me, clearly confused. "What are you doing here?" he finally asked.

"We wanted your barbecue alligator recipe," Ida Belle said. "We heard it was the best but your bar isn't exactly the kind of place we frequent."

"We were flying the drone ahead of us and saw Buck pull a gun on you," I said.

"We got closer to see if we could help and there was all this yelling," Gertie said. "Then everything got very confusing."

"No shit," Whiskey said.

Carter raised an eyebrow, and we knew he wasn't fooled for a minute. Fortunately, Whiskey was still in shock so he didn't even ask why I'd walked out of the bar instead of around the side with Ida Belle and Gertie.

A groan sounded beside me and Whiskey's eyes widened. I dropped down beside Buck and pushed him over. The wound in his side was seeping blood, but when I ripped his shirt open, I could tell it had probably missed major organs.

"He's losing blood fast," I said.

"I thought he was dead," Whiskey said.

I nodded. Buck hadn't moved a quarter of an inch since buckling over onto the ground. I figured he'd passed out, then bled out. I was happy to be wrong.

"Trevor forced you to buy the alligator meat, didn't he?" Carter asked.

Whiskey nodded. "He caught me poaching a gator. Not for bar sales. Just one for me and Pops. He said he'd make me an offer I couldn't refuse—he'd provide the gator, I'd sell it and give him eighty percent of the profit, and he wouldn't arrest me for poaching."

"How long has it been going on?" Carter asked.

"A couple months," Whiskey said. "He said he was leaving the state soon, so I thought it was almost over. I swear, I didn't know nothing about him doing that to Petey. Not until last night."

"You said you had proof?" Carter asked.

"I don't know how good it will be, but I marked the bills I paid him with. Put my initials on all of them. It's not much but I figured he didn't have any reason to have a stack of hundreds with my initials on it, so maybe somebody would look into it."

"You can bet on it, although I think you've got plenty of witnesses."

"Not just witnesses," Gertie said. "We have it on film. The drone got lodged in a tree behind us but the camera was directed right at Trevor. It was recording the entire time."

Gertie handed Carter Ida Belle's cell phone, then pulled her own out of her shirt pocket. "And if you need audio, I got a good bit of it here."

Whiskey looked over at Carter. "It's a good thing you showed up when you did or these ladies would have been turning it all over to you to work up murder charges. He was going to kill me."

Carter glanced over at me. "Something tells me you would have pulled through even if I'd been a little late to the party."

Whiskey may have missed my coming out of the bar, but Carter knew exactly why I'd been inside and what I'd been about to do. Carter was right—Whiskey would have made it out alive, but all of us would have been put through the wringer with the state. It was one thing for one law enforcement officer to shoot another in the line of duty. It was completely another thing for a civilian to do so.

I frowned. And now that Whiskey had mentioned Carter showing up to save the day, I wondered why Carter was there. Was he following up on the boat theft and just happened to show up at the right time, or was he working another angle of the poacher investigation as we were? I was just about to ask when I heard the siren in the distance.

"You guys can go ahead and get out of here," Carter said to me. "You'll just be in the way and I can get your statements later. I'll just take the phones, if you don't mind."

And that's when it hit me. My name would be in a report.

Carter would be investigated for shooting a state employee, especially another law enforcement officer. I'd be asked to give my story and the name Sandy-Sue Morrow would all be part of a homicide record. CIA Director Morrow would officially have a hemorrhage.

Then a thought occurred to me and I looked over at Whiskey.

"Say, given that you have the video, audio, and a cop and two women to vouch for you, do you think maybe you could forget I was ever here? I sorta have ongoing issues with cops, present company included."

Carter covered his mouth and coughed, and I could tell he was trying not to smile.

Whiskey frowned, then nodded. "You sure don't look like you'd be a lot of trouble, but I guess you never know. Far be it from me to put you on radar. Like you said, I got enough to cover me already and I don't know you from Adam anyway. As far as I'm concerned, I ain't never seen you before."

"Awesome," I said. "I owe you one."

"Let's get out of here," Ida Belle said, then looked at Carter. "You'll be letting Quincy and Petey out of jail, right?"

Carter nodded. "I'll call Deputy Breaux and tell him to do it right now."

Gertie handed Carter her phone, and we took off from the bar before Carter or Whiskey changed their minds or Buck got lucid and saw us all standing there. We made a quick hike back to the airboat, all talking over one another as we tried to make sense of everything that had gone down. So many answers, and yet, still so many questions, and with Trevor dead, we might not ever get an explanation for everything.

"I don't know that I'm cut out for this," I said as we climbed in the boat. "We had the wrong guy, and would have played right into Trevor's hands by pointing the finger at Whiskey."

Ida Belle frowned. "Don't be so hard on yourself. No one said this would be easy, and besides, even if we'd told Carter what we suspected, he wouldn't have taken our word for it. He would have collected more evidence before making an arrest. We were moving in the right direction. We just missed a jog in the road is all."

"I guess. But I still don't feel like we accomplished much."

"We did have a boat and car chase," Gertie said. "We didn't get to shoot anyone, but at least those have to count for something."

I smiled. "You know, I'm okay with not having to shoot anyone."

Ida Belle clapped me on the back. "Progress."

Chapter Nineteen

We went straight to Quincy's house when we got back to Sinful. Ida Belle and Gertie filled Quincy in on what had happened at the Swamp Bar, swearing him to secrecy, especially the part about me being there. He'd looked a bit confused but apparently figured it was something he was better off not asking about. Besides, he was so happy that he and Petey were back home and all the charges were dropped that he'd probably have forgotten his first name if we requested it.

I found a head shot of Trevor on the state's website and showed it to Petey. He frowned.

"Man in boat," he said. "In my boat. I told he was in my boat."

I looked at Quincy. "Did he tell you someone was in his boat?"

Quincy frowned. "About a month ago, he came home aggravated, but I checked the boat and nothing looked out of order. Maybe the warden was getting his ducks in a row for if he had to throw suspicion?"

I shrugged. "Maybe."

I looked at Petey. "Was the man in the boat the man who hurt the alligators?"

Petey shook his head and dropped his gaze to his chest. I asked again, but this time he drew his knees up to his chest, wrapped his arms around them, and started humming. I tried asking him more questions, but he'd gone to whatever that other place was and we couldn't get another word out of him.

After Quincy's we headed to our respective homes, anxious for a hot shower and much-needed rest. Ida Belle and Gertie would have to give Carter statements sometime later, but I imagined he would be wrapped up for a while telling his side of the story to the state. They weren't going to be happy with the end to this poaching case.

I took a long, hot shower, changed into shorts and a T-shirt and left off the bra, then headed outside for my hammock with a book and a beer. I'd earned a little relaxation, and I always thought better outside. This entire poaching mess had made me question whether or not being a private investigator was a good fit for me. Sure, I had the physical ability, knew the equipment, and could handle any form of combat and probably come out the winner ninety-nine times out of a hundred, but I was weak on making that leap from clues to who did it.

Since I'd been in Sinful and been getting into police business with Ida Belle and Gertie, there had been too many times I'd thought one thing and the truth had zigzagged the other direction. I thought my intuition was good, but I'd totally missed Trevor as the poacher. Granted, I hadn't liked him either time we'd had contact, but I hadn't made the leap from douche bag to criminal. So could I get better? How did Carter figure it all out? Although Gertie, Ida Belle, and I managed to be in the middle of things, especially at the final showdown scene, so to speak, often Carter was already ahead of us in putting his finger on the bad guy.

Like this time.

Now that I thought about it, was Carter at the bar because he suspected Whiskey, or had he already wondered about Trevor? Or had Whiskey really called Carter and told him he needed to talk, as he'd claimed? Then I remembered the comment Carter made about the state suspecting him of poaching and that it wouldn't be the first time law enforcement was the guilty party. Maybe I'd let Trevor fly under my radar because of his credentials. Maybe those same credentials made Carter do exactly the opposite.

Which made being a better investigator a matter of experience and not necessarily innate ability. I mean, you had to have some ability, clearly, or you wouldn't last a day. But would I get better with time? Unfortunately, there was only one way to answer that question, and that was to stick my nose into sheriff's department business again as soon as I got a chance.

I finally dropped the book to my chest and closed my eyes, too tired to make sense of it all. It felt as if I'd just dozed off when I heard a boat motor that sounded as though it was right next to me. I opened one eye and saw that the sun was going down and Carter was pulling up onto the bank in my backyard.

"Wow," I said. "I had a really long nap."

"Lucky," he said as he jumped onshore. "I had a really long afternoon. I don't suppose you'd take pity on a tired lawman and fix him a sandwich."

"Are you going to yell at me for being at the Swamp Bar?"

"Depends on how good the sandwich is."

"I have Gertie's roast beef and accept that challenge."

He groaned. Everyone knew Gertie made the best roast beef in Sinful. Even better than Francine's.

"You're not fighting fair," he said.

"That was your idea, not mine."

We headed for the kitchen and I made him a sandwich. I waited until he'd taken a bite before launching into the questions that had been building in my mind all afternoon.

"Did you already suspect Trevor before you went to the

Swamp Bar?" I asked.

"I had my suspicions."

"Why?"

He raised one eyebrow. "I assume you and the Troublesome Twosome thought Whiskey was the guilty party and you were there to get the dirt on him and save Petey?"

Since that's exactly what we were doing, and we had failed miserably, his summation made me a little testy.

"So what if we were?" I asked. "Defense attorneys hire people to find alternative theories to help get their clients off. So if there was a better suspect…"

"Petey doesn't have an attorney."

"Quincy hired us."

He raised an eyebrow. "Money exchanged hands?"

"Not exactly. It was more of an exchange of words."

He sighed. "I won't bother with the whole *you could have been killed, why were you in the middle of my investigation*, because I'm too tired to bang my head against that brick wall again. I *will* say I'm glad for the video and audio. When I presented them to the state, they walked quietly out the door. That wouldn't have happened if it had just been my word and Whiskey's. He's not exactly credible."

"What about Buck?"

"More credible than Whiskey, but the defense would have argued that he got confused after being shot and got it all wrong."

"Then he's going to be all right?"

Carter nodded. "The bullet missed everything major. He lost a good amount of blood and won't be shrimping anytime soon, but he should have a full recovery."

"That's good. I wasn't on the video, was I?"

"No, the camera was facing the swamp after it hit Trevor,

and Gertie cut off the audio before you came out of the bar."

Relief coursed through me. One less thing to worry about. "So again, why did you think it was Trevor?"

"I didn't think it was him, for certain. I just didn't think things were lining up right. The anonymous phone call, Petey being set up, Trevor still hanging around after his big arrest… I've been around the guy at law enforcement conferences. He was a gambler and a blowhole."

I frowned. "What do those have to do with poaching?"

"First of all, he didn't leave immediately after the arrest so he could start bragging to his coworkers at the main office. That would have been his usual MO. Why hang around here? Since that seemed a little odd and I knew about the gambling, I made some calls and found out that Trevor owed some not-so-nice people a good amount of money."

"That's it? You made the leap to poacher from that?"

"No. I made the leap from inconsistent behavior to needing money, and from that, I thought it warranted looking into. I was checking out Whiskey as well. His recent barbecue alligator plates had raised suspicion, but I hadn't figured on Trevor strong-arming Whiskey into selling his illegal goods."

"You thought Whiskey was poaching the alligator he was selling, like we did."

"That's the most logical train of thought, but Whiskey wouldn't have bothered with small gators, and even though he'll probably never be one of Sinful's upstanding citizens, I couldn't see him trying to pin it on Petey."

"Did Whiskey really call you like he told Buck?"

Carter nodded. "He wouldn't tell me anything over the phone so I figured I'd head over there and see what was up. I was coming up the channel near the highway when I saw Trevor's car turn off on the road to the Swamp Bar. Since there's nothing else down that road, I figured there was only one place he was going so I cut my engine down the channel and paddled up, hoping I could get evidence on one or both of them."

"You still thought Whiskey could be involved?"

"I had no reason not to. I knew something had spooked him, but that didn't mean he wasn't in the thick of it. So it could have been a partner meeting, or given what happened at the bar last night, I figured Trevor might be setting up his next fall guy."

"I wonder why Trevor tried to frame Petey first? I mean, clearly he was going to switch his plan to Whiskey based on the skin Buck found in his boat, but why not do that from the beginning?"

"I don't think Trevor was trying to frame Petey. I think he was using Petey's boat to do the poaching. He couldn't exactly run around in the state's boat, but they use the same launch where Petey's boat is kept. He probably saw that it never moved, ran the tags, and asked around. When I checked the boat, it was clear that it had been recently moved in and out of the slot several times. The grass around the wheels was starting to brown from the tires rolling over it."

"Quincy said Petey told him someone was in his boat, but when he checked it, everything seemed fine."

"And it probably was. Trevor was probably taking everything out of the boat when he used it. Maybe after a while he got lazy or complacent, or maybe since he was getting ready to cut and run, he figured if anyone noticed the stuff, they'd assume it was Petey's."

"Do you think there was ever an anonymous phone call? Or was Trevor just setting up his exit?"

Carter shrugged. "I don't think we'll ever know for sure."

I frowned. "There's something else I don't understand. If Trevor needed the money, why would he bother killing small gators?"

"If I had to guess, I'd say greed. He should have known how to get a smaller gator off a line without killing it. He probably figured it all added up, especially since he had Whiskey peddling his wares at well above market. The guys he was into money for don't play around."

"I guess that's why he was moving to Florida for another job."

"Probably one of many reasons, but he was stupid to go around announcing it. So you want to tell me what turned you guys onto Whiskey?"

"Oh, some friend of a friend of Gertie's told her about the barbecue gator. Said he was claiming it was some kind of special cut and charging a fortune for it. Ida Belle thought it sounded odd and that's how we ended up at the bar."

Hey, it wasn't a complete lie. I was Ida Belle's friend and had told her about the barbecue gator, and she told Gertie. So ultimately, the information did come from a friend of a friend of Gertie's. The last thing I'd offer up was that we'd been the ones to cause the fray at the Swamp Bar the night before, especially when we'd already lied and said we weren't there. And I certainly wasn't going to admit that Gertie had stolen a boat…again.

Carter finished up the sandwich, let out a huge sigh, and leaned back in his chair. "I'm just glad it's over. Maybe I can catch a break on crime until the results of the election audit are announced."

"What happens if Celia is still mayor?"

"Honestly? I'll start considering my options. I can't deal with four years of her. I'd shoot her before the first one was over."

"I would have shot her already."

He grinned. "Maybe while you're thinking about your future

plans, leave out law enforcement as a career. We don't get to kill everyone we don't like."

"A bullet probably wouldn't kill her either, unless it was silver and shaped into a cross."

He laughed. "You're going to keep me on my toes, aren't you?"

"On your toes and probably a whole lot of aggravated. Still interested?"

"God help me. Yes."

He rose from his chair and leaned over, kissing me soundly. Then he straightened up and stretched. "I've got to take Ida Belle's and Gertie's statements. I appreciate you asking Whiskey to leave you out of it. It saves me having to lie on paperwork again. I would love to tell you I'd be back to spend some quality time together when I'm done, but I'm pretty sure that time would be me sleeping. Don't get me wrong, it will be quality, but not the kind I have in mind to share with you."

I rose from my chair gave him a slap on the butt. "Get going. I'll be here when you're rested."

"I was thinking about grilling steaks tomorrow…a romantic dinner. Maybe you'd want to pack a toothbrush. Pajamas are optional but not encouraged."

I knew what he was offering, and it was a whole lot more than just a steak. Was I ready? I'd been over this moment in my mind a million times already and I'd never come up with an answer. But now, standing here in my kitchen and looking at him, I couldn't imagine saying no. I had no idea what the future held in store for me, but the one thing I did know was that I wanted Carter to be part of it.

"I love to have a romantic dinner sans pajamas with you," I said.

He smiled, and I could see the tiny bit of relief in his

expression. He'd been worried I'd turn him down. He reached out and gathered me in his arms and kissed me again. This time my legs went weak.

"Promise me something?" he said when he pulled back from the kiss.

"Sure."

"Don't get into any trouble between now and tomorrow."

"I'll give it my best shot."

"That's what I'm afraid of."

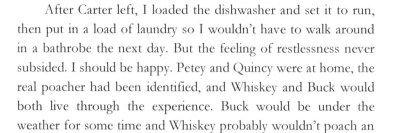

After Carter left, I loaded the dishwasher and set it to run, then put in a load of laundry so I wouldn't have to walk around in a bathrobe the next day. But the feeling of restlessness never subsided. I should be happy. Petey and Quincy were at home, the real poacher had been identified, and Whiskey and Buck would both live through the experience. Buck would be under the weather for some time and Whiskey probably wouldn't poach an alligator again for a while, but it could have been a lot worse for both of them.

But something still bothered me.

Everything Carter proposed was completely plausible and probably what happened, but with Trevor dead, we might never know the entire truth of the matter. Not for certain. Carter had laid it all out logically, and I was nothing if not logical. So why was it bothering me so much to not know for sure? Why couldn't I let this go?

I walked into the pantry to grab a roll of paper towels and reached for it on the top shelf. Next to the paper towels was a set of glass jars—jellies and pickles that Gertie had made and given to me. My gaze locked on the pickle jar and suddenly everything made sense.

I forgot the paper towels and headed straight for my Jeep.

It was late evening when I parked in front of Ramona's house. I walked up onto the porch and knocked on the front door.

"It's Fortune," I called out. "Marge's niece."

I heard movement inside and a couple seconds later, the door opened and Ramona peered out the crack. When she saw it was me, she opened the door and indicated I should come inside.

"I just opened a bottle of wine," she said. "Can I offer you a glass?"

"That would be great." I took a seat in the living room and a minute later, Ramona returned with two glasses of wine and took a seat in a chair across from me.

"I can't tell you how happy I was to hear that Petey and Quincy were back at home where they belong," Ramona said.

"Me too."

She frowned. "It was surprising…finding out the game warden was the poacher."

I nodded. "I don't think anyone saw that one coming, except maybe Carter. He was a step ahead of all of us on this one."

"That's not necessarily a bad thing. After all, it's his job. You guys were just helping out."

"True. And that's why I'm here now."

"What do you mean?"

I looked her straight in the eyes. "You have to stop."

She stared at me for a long time, never blinking, then finally lowered her gaze to the floor. "How did you know?"

"I didn't know for sure until now, but I suspected. It never made sense to me that Trevor would kill small gators. Why run the risk for less profit, especially given his position with the state? But someone who didn't have the strength Trevor did might go for a smaller kill."

She didn't agree with me, but she didn't argue with me either, so I continued.

"And although I believe Petey saw Trevor in the boat," I said, "I don't think he saw Trevor poaching. I think he saw you, and that's why he goes into that hiding place in his mind whenever I ask him who hurt the alligators."

She sighed. "I know it seems stupid, but when I saw Petey getting closer and closer to the water, I panicked. I couldn't lose him, too. I couldn't watch Quincy live through what I did."

"You can't kill them all," I said quietly.

"I know. I've always known. I just had to do something, and I didn't know what else to do."

I felt awful for her. I knew that feeling of hopelessness—of wanting so badly to do something that made a difference but not having any idea what that something was. I'd felt that way when my mother died.

"What happened to your son was horrible," I said. "Probably the most horrible thing that can ever happen to a person, but my understanding is that it's not that common. I know it's not a guarantee, but the odds of the same thing happening to Petey are really low."

Ramona sniffed and nodded. "I know you're right. I've lived here all my life and understand as well as the next guy how gators behave. The odds are against it, but the more I thought about Petey standing that close to the bayou, the more panicked I got."

"I understand."

She rubbed her nose with her finger. "Can I ask a favor?"

"Sure."

"Before you turn me in, will you give me some time to explain it all to Quincy? He's important and I don't want him thinking less of me than he has to."

I stared at her, a bit surprised. "I'm not turning you in. I would never turn you in."

Her eyes widened. "Aren't you dating Deputy LeBlanc?"

"Yeah, but I don't work for him. I'm under no professional obligation to report anything."

"What about a moral one?"

"The moral obligation is why I'm *here*."

Her eyes misted up, and she looked down at the floor again. I could tell she was embarrassed.

"You're a good woman," she said. "Your aunt would have been very proud of you."

"Thank you," I said. The comment pleased me. What little I knew about Marge were all things I respected.

Ramona rose from her chair and went over to the painting on the wall that I'd admired the first time we visited. She lifted it off the hook and handed it to me.

"I want you to have this," she said. "As a thank-you and as a show of friendship. I've been hiding in this swamp for a long time now. Maybe it's time that changed."

I took the painting and looked down at it, still amazed with the beauty contained on a piece of canvas.

"I don't know what to say," I said. "It's incredible. Thank you."

"I know you'll appreciate it. I could tell how much you loved it the first time you saw it." She stopped talking for a couple seconds, then started again. "Ida Belle and Gertie will know where you got it and they'll want to know why."

"And I'll tell them. But don't worry. Your secrets are always safe with those two."

Ramona nodded. "People say they're the town busybodies, but I think there's a whole lot beneath those surfaces."

"You have no idea."

Chapter Twenty

The next morning, Ida Belle, Gertie, and I sat in my kitchen, eating blackberry cobbler with mimosas. They'd been late at the sheriff's department the night before, giving Carter their statements, but it looked as though the entire thing was going to end there. The state hadn't requested that they speak to anyone involved, probably wanting to put the entire embarrassing mess behind them as soon as possible.

"It's a lot to take in," Ida Belle said. "So much happened so quickly. I tossed and turned most of the night just trying to process it all."

"We didn't do such a great job, did we?" I asked. "We had the wrong guy pegged as the poacher and completely overlooked the real one."

"In our defense," Gertie said, "that was one we didn't see coming."

"Of course we didn't see it coming," I said, "but that's my point. Carter did. Or he had his suspicions, anyway, and that was loads more than we had."

"Give yourself a break," Ida Belle said. "Carter's been doing this for a while, and he has the added advantage of knowing most of the players. If he hadn't known Trevor on a personal basis, he wouldn't have known his behavior was off."

"That's true," I said, slightly mollified. "I guess I just have to keep working at it."

"That," Gertie said, "and you have to stick around Sinful long enough to get a fix on everyone."

I laughed. "I'm not sure a hundred years would be enough time to get a fix on Sinful."

"She's got a point," Ida Belle said. "We've lived here all our lives and we've still had a couple surprises lately."

Gertie nodded. "I guess we'll never know about the anonymous phone call. What do you think, Fortune?"

I shrugged. "The most likely explanation is that Trevor saw Petey in the boat with his equipment and figured he'd better cut his losses. He would have been long gone before the case fell apart."

I frowned. Once again, it was the most logical explanation, but I'd never been completely satisfied with it.

"What?" Ida Belle asked. "You thinking it was someone else?"

"Not really," I said, "it was just something I wondered about."

"What?" Gertie asked.

"Could Petey have made that phone call?" I asked. "When we showed him the picture of Trevor, he said he'd told. Maybe he didn't just mean Quincy."

Ida Belle and Gertie both frowned.

"I don't know," Gertie said, "but it's an interesting theory. I think Petey is a lot more capable than people think. But if he made the call, he wouldn't have realized that the man he was reporting it to was the same man he was reporting on."

"That would suck," I said. "If Petey had caused the ball to drop on himself without even knowing it."

Gertie nodded. "I can't believe it was Ramona killing the smaller gators." She stabbed a hunk of cobber.

"I can," Ida Belle said. "Ramona was never a lightweight. If she made up her mind to do something, she was going to do it. And given the way she feels about Quincy and Petey, I'd guess she was more motivated than the average person."

"Hey," I said, "you don't think Ramona and Quincy are a thing, do you?"

Ida Belle looked a bit surprised, then shrugged. "I don't think so, but I can see it happening."

"They would make a good couple," Gertie said. "They both prefer being inside and left alone and they're both dedicated to Petey. I wonder if Quincy's ever considered it."

"Uh-oh," Ida Belle said. "I know that look."

"What look?" Gertie asked, trying to act innocent and failing completely.

"That look you get when you're going to play matchmaker," Ida Belle said. "Just stay out of it. If it's meant to be then it will be."

"Really?" Gertie said. "And what proof do you have to back that one up? You and Walter are still single, and Fortune can't manage to jump on the best-looking guy in town. Who, I might add, would have no problem with the jumping part."

"You don't know that for certain," Ida Belle said.

Gertie threw her hands in the air. "He's young and good-looking. She's young and good-looking. No one's married, ill, or gay."

"Maybe she's being cautious," Ida Belle said. "I know you don't understand caution, but the rest of the world doesn't rush into things like you do."

"I'd settle for a slow crawl," Gertie said. "Maybe even a belly scoot."

I leaned back in my chair and relaxed. I wasn't about to tell her about my romantic dinner tonight with Carter, especially the part about a toothbrush but no pajamas. She'd pester me for details until the cows came home, and that was something I couldn't ever see being comfortable doing. Gertie was going to have to settle for a big grin. If Carter was as good at pajama-less sleepovers as he was at everything else, I predicted I'd be wearing one for a while.

But right now, I was going to enjoy a little peace and quiet. No pressure to perform. No worry about injustice. Just three women having some mimosas and excellent baked goods. Everything was calm. Maybe not for long. Maybe not even until we finished the cobbler. But for now, I was relaxing in my kitchen with my two best friends and listening to them argue about my love life.

No gunshots. No explosions. No fire.

My cell phone rang and I looked at it. Carter.

"Speak of the devil," I said, and answered.

"Mr. Walker just called in a report of an alligator stealing an apple pie that was cooling on his back porch steps," Carter said. "And in other news, you've been accused of stealing cookies from a toddler."

I grinned. The calm was over, but now we were back to normal.

More adventures with Fortune and the girls coming in 2017!

About the Author

Jana DeLeon grew up among the bayous and gators of southwest Louisiana. She's never stumbled across a mystery like one of her heroines but is still hopeful. She lives in Dallas, Texas with a menagerie of animals and not a single ghost.

Visit Jana at:

Website: http://janadeleon.com

Facebook: http://www.facebook.com/JanaDeLeonAuthor/

Twitter: @JanaDeLeon